CROSSINGLINES

OTHER BOOKS BY PAUL VOLPONI:

CROSSINGLINES

Paul Volponi

VIKING

An Imprint of Penguin Group (USA) Inc.

VIKING
Published by Penguin Group
Penguin Group (USA) Inc., 345 Hudson Street, New York, New York 10014, U.S.A.
Penguin Group (Canada), 90 Eglinton Avenue East, Suite 700, Toronto, Ontario,
Canada M4P 2Y3 (a division of Pearson Penguin Canada Inc.)
Penguin Books Ltd, 80 Strand, London WC2R 0RL, England
Penguin Ireland, 25 St Stephen's Green, Dublin 2, Ireland
(a division of Penguin Books Ltd)
Penguin Group (Australia), 250 Camberwell Road, Camberwell, Victoria 3124,
Australia (a division of Pearson Australia Group Pty Ltd)
Penguin Books India Pvt Ltd, 11 Community Centre, Panchsheel Park,
New Delhi – 110 017, India
Penguin Group (NZ), 67 Apollo Drive, Rosedale, Auckland 0632, New Zealand
(a division of Pearson New Zealand Ltd.)
Penguin Books (South Africa) (Pty) Ltd, 24 Sturdee Avenue, Rosebank,
Johannesburg 2196, South Africa

Penguin Books Ltd, Registered Offices: 80 Strand, London WC2R 0RL, England

First published in 2011 by Viking, a member of Penguin Group (USA) Inc.

10 9 8 7 6 5 4 3 2 1

LIBRARY OF CONGRESS CATALOGING-IN-PUBLICATION DATA
Volponi, Paul.
Crossing lines / by Paul Volponi.
p. cm.
Summary: High school senior Adonis struggles to do the right thing when his fellow
football players escalate their bullying of a new classmate, Alan, who is transgendered.
ISBN 978-0-670-01214-5 (hardcover)
[1. Conduct of life—Fiction. 2. Transgender people—Fiction. 3. Bullies—Fiction.
4. Football—Fiction. 5. Family life—Fiction. 6. High schools—Fiction.
7. Schools—Fiction.] I. Title.
PZ7.V8877Cr 2011   [Fic]—dc22   2010033292

Printed in USA   Set in Horley Old Style   Book design by Kate Renner
Blaze logo by Sabrina Volponi

THIS BOOK IS DEDICATED TO THOSE WHO ARE BRAVE
ENOUGH TO SET ASIDE WHAT THEY'VE BEEN TOLD
AND DECIDE FOR THEMSELVES WHAT IS RIGHT.

———

Special Thanks to Joy Peskin, Regina Hayes,
Rosemary Stimola, April Volponi, Jim Cocoros,
Mary Volponi, and Sabrina Volponi.

CROSSINGLINES

"We all got holes to fill."

— TOWNES VAN ZANDT

SOMETIMES YOUR SHOES CAN BE FILLED WITH

garbage, and you don't even know it. I understand that now. That it can take a long time to get your stuck-up nose down to where it belongs, down to where you can smell your own stink.

The first time I ever laid eyes on Alan was late last May, in gym class. Junior year.

It was during the warm-up, and we were all running laps around the red rubber track circling the athletic field.

I was pushing myself to keep pace with Rodney Bishop and James Godfrey, two speedy wide receivers on the football team with me. We were coming up quick on Alan from behind, as his blond hair bounced against his bony shoulder blades. He must have heard our footsteps coming, because he cut from the inside lane onto the grass to let us go past.

"Oh, shit! Did you see that fag?" asked Bishop, real loud. "I swear, I thought that new kid was gonna be a chick from behind."

"Yeah, you were about to holler at that homo and ask him out," cracked Godfrey.

I looked back over my shoulder and saw that Alan had stopped.

I knew he'd heard Bishop, and I thought that expression on his face—somewhere between being really pissed off and ready to cry—was funny as hell.

"Nah, I knew that was a faggot all along," Bishop defended himself. "How 'bout you, Adonis? Did you know?"

"Are you kidding?" I said as we leaned into the turn, three abreast. "I knew from fifty yards back. That's why he runs so slow. His butt hurts."

"That why *you've* been getting slower?" Godfrey cackled at Bishop. "Your butt hurts, too?"

"That's *you*. I'll show you slow," Bishop said, turning on the jets and pulling away.

Godfrey sprinted after him.

I tried to go with them. But a big offensive lineman like me couldn't keep up, and they just left me in their dust.

Alan had just transferred into Central High, and I'd

have called it a rough beginning. I remember some of the other guys taking jabs at Alan, making comments about his tight-ass pants, asking him if he'd transferred from a high school in San Francisco, or calling him a fag to his face.

I had run my mouth at him a few times, too, even though he never did anything to me or anybody else I knew.

Other than that one time on the running track, I never saw Alan let a nasty remark go.

He'd usually come right back at you with a sharp tongue, waving his finger around and saying things like, "If you want to be judge and jury, you should stand in front of the mirror more. That way you can talk to the source of your problem."

He even called a cafeteria table full of football players I was sitting at "pigs," when one of us whistled at him as a joke.

That kind of insult was almost funny coming from him, like *he* had the right to put himself over anybody.

After that, whenever guys on the team saw Alan, we'd scrunch up our snouts like pigs and snort at him.

Then the teachers and deans couldn't get on us for using "inappropriate" language.

I was convinced that hostility between Alan and the football team was all Alan's fault.

He could be gay if he wanted. There were probably some other kids at our school who were *that way*, too, or leaning there.

But they didn't make a show out of it, like Alan did. So nobody really cared.

He didn't have to flit around the hallways drawing attention to himself, swinging his hips and arms like a raging fem.

And whatever shit Alan took on account of it, I figured he deserved.

Alan didn't have problems with most of the girls at school. I guess that's because he was almost one of them. He'd usually be hanging around with a group of females, even good-looking ones. That got a lot of *real* guys even more annoyed, feeling like they couldn't go over and make a move on one of them with him there. It would be too weird.

When school broke for the summer, at the end of

June, I didn't see Alan again for a couple of months.

I didn't know what dudes like him did with their vacations. Maybe he was sitting in the library all day. Maybe he got a summer job serving cappuccino in a coffeehouse, or was at home plucking his eyebrows. Or maybe he hung around some men's room in a public park waiting to hook up with another queer.

I just knew wherever Alan was, I wasn't.

And that was perfect with me.

1

I didn't see Alan again until early September. It was the Tuesday after Labor Day, on the first day of our senior year.

He was in my English and gym classes, first and last period, every day.

I made sure to sit on the other side of the room from him in English. And in gym, I was safe because I changed my clothes in the section of lockers reserved for varsity athletes, where I'd been changing for two years already, and where Alan was nowhere in sight.

I never figured on Alan jumping up into my life past being in those two classes. But he did.

It was just after one o'clock, but the first day of school was already over. We'd had a half day, with twenty-minute classes to get our program cards signed. I was walking across the athletic field with some of my teammates, heading towards the weight room—a beat-up trailer that used to store textbooks before it got converted into something useful. We were going to pump some serious iron and get ready for our first football game of the season the following week, after putting in a month of practices in the heat of August.

"Spy what's up on the bleachers," Bishop said. "It's Chick City. Just look at all those lovelies. There must be forty of them."

"Is that some kind of meeting they're having?" asked Ethan, our quarterback and team captain. "I don't remember them asking my permission. It's never good when that many girls get together. All they do is compare notes and bitch about us."

Ethan was six foot two, the same height as me. Only he already had the kind of body I was lifting weights to get. His shoulders were as wide as mine, but his waist was probably seven inches smaller, and his muscles were really cut.

Almost every girl I ever heard pass a comment about

him used the word *hot*, even if they did call him a prick, too.

And that's what I wanted.

"They're probably deciding how far to go on a first date," said Godfrey.

"Send 'em a memo from me—it's either all the way or the highway," said Ethan, pounding a football between his huge paws. "I got a no-tease policy."

"Yeah, put out or get out of the car and walk home," echoed Godfrey. "No middle ground on that."

Right away, my eyes settled on Melody Singer, a senior, who was sitting in the second row. I'd hung out with her a few times over the summer.

The first time was with a bunch of other kids, including my sister, Jeannie, who was a year younger than me. Jeannie understood that I had it bad for Melody, so she set it up for me to tag along to this lightweight kegger. I was the only jock in the crowd, so I knew I'd stood out. Hardly anybody there, except for me, had more than two small cups of beer. And no one puked or got loud.

I spent the whole night zeroed in on Melody, paying

attention to what she said about a bunch of books I'd never read and the kind of movies I hadn't seen.

I'd wanted to get next to Melody for a long time. It was more than her just being pretty. She was smart, too. And there was something about Melody I couldn't explain, something that jumped up and hit me over the head every time I laid eyes on her. But she usually had more guys falling over her than I could count. So the competition was always stiff, and I'd never made a real move on her before.

Besides, I'd heard her say around school, "Football players and wrestlers are basically pinheads. I don't like guys whose attitudes are bigger than their brains."

But I knew that Jeannie had put in a good word for me, and I made sure to agree with everything Melody said that night about those books and movies, even though I had to fake it.

It all paid off for me a few days later, when Melody pulled into the service station where I had a summer job. She'd just got her license and her parents had bought her a used Chevy Cavalier.

"It has a few little hiccups," Melody told me, wrapping some strands of her long brown hair around a finger. "The previous owner said something about plugs and belts needing to be changed soon. Only I'm not exactly sure which ones. I'm totally clueless about anything that takes a screwdriver or a wrench."

"Listen, don't fall into that stereotype of good-looking women not knowing anything about their rides," I pitched her through the open driver's window as I gassed up her tank. "It's not about being a grease monkey. It's all high-tech now. Car mechanics is a science. If you want, I could come by your place and teach you some of the basics."

I didn't know how much of that rap I really believed. But it got me an afternoon alone with Melody in her driveway. Then a couple of movie dates after that, where I first slipped my arm around her, tasted those sweet lips, and took a walk with my hands as far as she'd let me.

Suddenly, every one of those girls on the bleachers began clapping over something.

"Thank you, ladies! Thank you!" yelled Bishop, without missing a beat. "I appreciate your worship!"

There were a few laughs from the bleachers, and even a sarcastic, "You're *not* welcome!"

Just then those girls started getting up to leave.

That's when Melody saw me, and began waving.

I bolted across the field towards her with the smell of the fresh-cut grass filling my lungs.

"Adonis, look up!" Ethan shouted, a second before he zipped me a pass.

I caught that pigskin in full stride and ran up to Melody with it tucked away beneath my left arm.

"So what's been going on here?" I asked her.

"First meeting of the Fashion Club," Melody answered with a wide pearly smile. "Big doings—we just elected officers."

"Oh, that's great," I said, trying to sound interested. "You know, lots of guys are into fashion, too. I know some of the most famous designers in the world are men."

"Yeah, you're right. They're some of my favorites— Ralph Lauren and Yves Saint Laurent. I'm pretty impressed you know that! Hey, I want you to meet someone," Melody said excitedly, reaching out to spin somebody around by the shoulder to face me. "Adonis, this is our new Fashion Club president, Alan."

Everything inside me tensed up as my eyes locked onto his. That shrimp was almost a foot shorter than I was. And even standing on the bottom row of the bleachers, Alan was only eye level with me.

"Oh, yes. Hello," he said, flipping the tail end of a long scarf around his neck, like he was Snoopy, that big-nosed dog from the *Peanuts* comics, ready to duel the Red Baron. "Adonis, you're in two of my classes, aren't you?"

It freaked me out that Alan knew that, like maybe he'd been watching my ass. Or even worse, he had some kind of man crush on me. But with Melody there, I was fighting back every instinct I had to snort at him.

"I'm not exactly sure," I answered.

"Well, it's a pleasure to *formally* meet you, Adonis," he said, extending his small pale hand. "Any friend of Melody's . . ."

I normally would have left a loser like him hanging out there. But I couldn't now. His grip felt so limp and clammy, I would have sworn I'd shoved my hand into a bowl of warm chowder.

"That's a very unusual name, Adonis," Alan said. "It comes from Greek mythology, doesn't it?"

I wasn't about to discuss anything *Greek* with Alan in public.

"Yeah, how did you get that name?" Melody asked.

"It was my mother's idea. She studied art, and there's some statue of a naked god with a perfect body named Adonis," I said, watching Melody look me over from head to toe. "My father liked it, too, because of his favorite wrestler growing up—'Adorable' Adrian Adonis, who was the tag-team champ."

That's when I heard a familiar voice call my name, and footsteps coming down the bleachers towards me.

"I believe you already know our vice president," Melody said.

I looked up and it was my sister Jeannie, who'd just become a junior.

"Since when do you care about fashion?" Jeannie asked, smirking from ear to ear. "I mean, besides what the cheerleaders are wearing?"

"I've got lots of interests you don't know about," I answered with some attitude.

"Adonis, aren't you going to congratulate your sister?" Melody asked, nudging my elbow. "Vice president's a big honor, and *I* nominated her."

"Sure I am," I said. "Congratulations, Jeannie."

"Oh, she's a sweetheart, this one. She'll do a great job," Alan said.

Then he kissed Jeannie on the cheek, with a long *mmmmm-waa*, and that was enough for me.

"Hey, I gotta go. We're weight training today," I said, and turned my back to a chorus of good-byes.

The guys were all standing at the door to the trailer, grinning at me. And I could feel my face getting redder and redder on the walk over.

"You were pretty friendly with gay boy there," said Bishop, with the rest of them already laughing. "What he want from you?"

"Nothing. He wants a date with *you* after we're finished," I answered, tossing him the football. "I told him you'd definitely be into it."

———

THAT NIGHT, MOM HAD TO CALL JEANNIE DOWN TO DINNER twice. The second time, she used that reverse-psychology crap on her.

"I don't care, stay on the phone!" Mom yelled upstairs, like she was playing the class of third-grade kids she taught. "Barclay's begging to trade his dog food for your pepper steak! I hope you like *Alpo!*"

The steam rose off the plate in front of me, and my stomach was rumbling to join my nostrils in that feast. But me and Dad both knew Mom would have pitched a fit if either one of us lifted a fork before we were all seated at the table.

"Jeannie, now!" Dad demanded. "Shake it or lose it!"

Dad was only home three nights a week from his job as a firefighter, and his number-one rule was six thirty dinner together.

"I grew up the youngest of seven kids. I barely knew my older brothers and sisters by the time they were out of the house," Dad had told me a hundred times over. "Your grandfather, God rest his soul, was a laborer. He came home exhausted every night, and never wanted to hear a word out of us while he was eating. So he was half a stranger to me, too. That's not going to happen in this family. I promise. I'm going to hear you. And you're going to know what I'm thinking."

"Call me back later then," Jeannie said, snapping her cell phone shut and stuffing it down into a pocket as she slid into her seat. "Sorry, Fashion Club business."

"Are they paying you?" Dad asked her.

"No. Why?" said Jeannie, sounding confused.

"Then it's not business and we're still your only bosses," Dad said, pointing back and forth between Mom and himself with the dull edge of a knife.

"Your daughter was elected vice president," said Mom.

"Hey, that's wonderful," Dad said. "I see all of that clothes shopping finally got you somewhere."

"Very funny, *ha-ha*," said Jeannie.

"I'm just kidding," Dad added under a glare from Mom. "That's great news."

"Dad, now get this, the president's the one dude in the club," I said, chewing on a piece of meat. "And he's gay."

"Well, who did you expect him to be, Tarzan of the Apes?" said Dad.

"You don't know for sure Alan's gay," Jeannie said.

"Why? Did he come on to you?" I asked her.

"No. Did he come on to *you?*" she rifled back.

"Oh, I forgot, *macho man* kissed you on the cheek," I said.

"Let it go, the two of you," Mom said. "I'll have you know your father kissed me on the cheek at the end of our first date."

"Yeah, but I was just reeling you in slow," said Dad. "Anyway, I have to trust my son on this one. I taught him to know the difference."

"Really?" said Jeannie. "And what kind of sick, homophobic lesson was that?"

"Is he, Adonis?" Dad asked, brushing off Jeannie's question.

Jeannie bit her lip hard, and I could tell Dad had gotten under her skin.

So I just let my wrist go limp in response, to really irk Jeannie.

"Do you believe them?" Jeannie asked Mom.

"This is how most men work out their fears," Mom answered. "It's almost like they never leave high school. Or is it *junior* high? I don't encourage it inside this house. But believe me, it's better than them doing it in public."

"Funny how Adonis had an interest in the Fashion Club when he was talking to Melody Singer," said Jeannie.

"Of course. He's a dog just like his old man," said Dad with a wide grin.

I liked hearing that so much I sneaked Barclay a strip of steak beneath the table.

"Are there any gay students in your school?" Mom asked.

"How should I know?" I answered.

"You *seem* to be keeping track," Jeannie said with her eyes on mine. "Not that I know of, Mom. I'm sure there are, though. They just don't advertise it."

"All right, that's enough gay talk," said Dad, stabbing at another piece of meat on his plate. "What exactly goes on in this Fashion Club, Jeannie? I know you're too old to play dress-up."

"I get a chance to show off my designs and get some feedback. I'm thinking that's what I might want to be, a fashion designer," she said. "But other girls have different goals. Some want to be models. Others girls just want to celebrate their sense of style."

"See, you said it, '*girls*,'" I sniped. "There are no *guys* in your club."

"Enough of that, Adonis," Mom said in a stern voice, gripping her water glass.

"How did your classes go?" asked Dad. "You know, the real reason you go to school, besides fashion and football."

Jeannie and me said, "Fine," almost in harmony, like we were part of the glee club.

"And how was your first day at school, Mom?" asked Jeannie.

"My students are all lovely, thirty-five little attention seekers who can't stop talking."

I thought how I could never be a teacher, and have a first day of school every year for the rest of my life.

Towards the end of dinner, Jeannie's phone rang.

She pulled it from her pocket and looked at the display.

"It's Alan," she said, pushing away her plate. "Mom, it's important. We need to come up with an agenda for tomorrow's meeting. And I'm done eating. Can I be excused?"

"Take it into the living room," Mom told her.

As Jeannie left the table, Dad called after her, "Let me talk to this Alan. I've got a question for him."

"No!" Jeannie hollered back.

"I just want to ask why he's calling during dinner hour," said Dad. "Doesn't *his* family share this time? 'Cause he's sure as hell interfering with ours."

2

Mr. D'Antoni, one of those long-haired hippie types with a ponytail, was our English teacher. You could be *different* like that if you were into poems and plays, and people wouldn't think much about it. I knew lots of girls at school worshiped D'Antoni over all that self-expression nonsense he preached. I'd had him for English before as a sophomore, and as a homeroom teacher, too. He could be a real pain, asking you to explain your answers fully, or talk about how a story made you feel deep inside. And he was always quoting some kind of stupid poetry about how the whole world could be found in a single leaf of grass. I figured that when it came to grass, D'Antoni probably got so strange by smoking plenty of it.

"We're going to start off the semester with a group

project," D'Antoni announced on the second day of school. "This may seem like a strange question for English class, but raise your hand if you know the names of at least ten sports teams."

My hand shot up right away. So did the hands of most kids, except for a few of the girls, and Alan.

"Good, we have a foundation of knowledge to begin with," said D'Antoni. "Does anybody know the nickname of the football team that plays in Baltimore?"

"Ravens!" I shouted, along with several other kids.

"That's right. But now I want you to all to think, how did they get that name?" D'Antoni asked.

There was about thirty seconds of near silence. Then one of the girls said, "Since this is English class, I'm going to guess it's got something to do with that poem 'The Raven.'"

"You're very correct," said D'Antoni. "Point of fact, Poe didn't write his famed poem 'The Raven' in Baltimore. He wrote it either in Philadelphia or New York, in eighteen forty-five, I believe. But he did die in Baltimore, in eighteen forty-nine, where he's still buried today. He was found delirious on the streets, dressed in someone else's clothes, hours before he died."

"Then why did Baltimore name their team after that poem, instead of New York or Philly?" someone else asked.

"His grave's a tourist attraction in Baltimore. It's a case of, We've got the body, we get to celebrate him," answered D'Antoni. "Now, what's the name of our school's sports teams?"

"Wildcats!" everybody said, even Alan.

Then a guy in the front row gave our school cheer, ripping his hand through the air, like his fingers were sharp claws, as he growled, *"Gggrrrrrrrrr!"*

"Why are we the Central High Wildcats?" D'Antoni asked. "Wildcats are native to Europe, Asia, and Africa, not anywhere around here."

Nobody had a real answer, and neither did D'Antoni.

"I looked it up," he said. "It's the most popular name of school teams in America. Other than that, I can't find a reason it should be ours. But I'll expect your groups, which will be comprised of four students, to use a little more creativity when you get assigned a city to research from one of these unmarked envelopes. Then you'll give that city a brand-new team, with a nickname, a sport to play, and a logo."

I was psyched to hear that was actually schoolwork.

Two of my teammates, Toby and Marshall, who played on the offensive line with me, were already looking over in my direction. I nodded to them. I was even considering the chunky girl sitting next to me, who never dated and was all about her grades, as a fourth, in case the three of us slacked off on whatever writing part there probably was to do.

Toby wasn't much of a student, and mostly got the kind of passing grades that teachers give you for showing up every day. As sad as it sounds, he helped pull Marshall along in school, double-teaming homework assignments. And I'd helped them both out last year, trying to keep our offensive line together and not flunking off the team.

I wasn't up for any academic awards either. But at least I knew what a B-plus looked like. I figured if I could get a decent grade in subjects I wasn't interested in, I'd be golden on any kind of sports project. And working with those guys would make the whole thing even more like fun and less like schoolwork.

Only D'Antoni put an end to all that.

"I don't want these groups to be made up of the regular cliques," he said. "This project's a beginning-of-the-semester icebreaker as much as it's an academic experience. So I'm going to use a number sequence, hopefully to create groups of students who normally don't work together."

There were twenty-eight kids in class, and D'Antoni had us count off from one to seven.

"Three," said Alan in a soft voice, when his turn came.

The odds were against it, so I just laughed at the thought of getting stuck with him in my group.

Then, as kids in the row next to mine counted off, the numbers added up fast inside my brain, and I knew I was about to be screwed.

I was ready to dive into another chair, to change the count.

But D'Antoni must have seen me start to move, because his eyes settled on mine, and I was stuck.

When it was my turn, I put every bit of bass into my voice that I could and said, "Three."

A minute later, chairs were sliding all around me as everyone moved to get into their groups. I sank down in my seat like I could ignore it, refusing to move. But in the end, Alan and two girls came over to where I was.

"Hello, Adonis," he said, way too happy and loud.

Toby and Marshall must have heard him, because they both snorted. Alan shot them a cold stare. I just kept my mouth shut and let their insults stand as my reply.

Maxine, one of the girls in our group, knew Alan from the Fashion Club. And I had to watch the two of them hug, kissing the air next to each other's cheeks.

That's when D'Antoni walked past us and said, "Perfect, two men and two women here."

I wanted to yank him back by the ponytail, telling that hippie to open his eyes and look again. That I was the only guy in this group.

"I'll bet Adonis is going to want to do a football team," Alan said.

"You think I want to *do* a football team?" I asked him, snide.

"Well, that's your favorite sport, isn't it?" he said.

"It's not about me. Maybe you want to *do* a football team. But I don't."

"Oh, I see. Would you like to *do* a women's football team, Adonis?" Alan asked with a smirk.

"I love synchronized swimming and gymnastics," Maxine interrupted. "Do those kinds of teams have names?"

And that little joust between me and Alan was finished.

D'Antoni explained to the class that two members of each group would research the history of the city we got assigned, and the other two would find out all about the sports people played around there, and the team names the city already had.

Then he called one student up from each group to pick an envelope. The city inside the one that Maxine chose for us was Cincinnati, Ohio.

"If it's all right, I'll do facts about the city," Alan said. "I love learning the history of places I've never been."

"Fine. I want to do the sports part," I said.

So Maxine and Alan became partners, and I worked with the other girl, Wendy.

Maxine was as cool as could be, always wearing some kind of funky outfit and different kinds of shades—big round ones, tiny ones that balanced on the tip of her nose, or glasses with the frames covered in glitter.

Wendy was the opposite. She dressed pretty plain and never made much noise. I recognized her from a few classes we'd had together. But I wasn't completely sure of her name until she said it.

"What a wonderful name," Alan told her when he first heard it. "That's from *Peter Pan*. It's one of my favorite stories."

"I hear that a lot, maybe too much," said Wendy. "I was never a big fan of the story. I always thought it was depressing—the way Wendy's parents treated her, and how Peter didn't want to grow up."

"Oh, don't think about it that way," said Alan. "Look for the magic in it, the freedom of flying wherever you want, in any world."

I figured Alan could be Tinker Bell, the way he flitted around. He was small enough. And all he was missing were the wings and the fairy dust.

Then Maxine said, "What if we dressed our sports team like Peter Pan?"

"Green tights and pointy shoes for uniforms. And one of those little caps with a tickle-me feather in it," said Alan. "Girl, you could be a fashion trendsetter."

"You're too late with that thought. I already *am* one," answered Maxine, winking at Alan.

"Wait, that's not the assignment, designing uniforms," said Wendy.

"That's right, it's not," I added.

I was about to be sick to my stomach, when D'Antoni made it even worse by handing out a poem.

"I think this one by Walt Whitman fits the circumstances of an icebreaker rather well," he said. "Read it in your groups and then discuss. See if you learn a little more about each other from it."

There was a picture of Whitman at the bottom of the page, and I understood why D'Antoni must have liked him so much. He looked like the world's biggest hippie, with a wild and filthy bird's nest for a beard. Besides that picture, the only thing I knew about Whitman was that his name was on the heart-shaped box of chocolates me and Jeannie chipped in to buy for Mom every Valentine's Day. It was called a "Whitman's Sampler."

"I'll read it," Alan told our group, without getting an argument, especially from me.

"'Are you the new person drawn toward me?'" he started off.

"To begin with take warning, I am surely far
different from what you suppose;
Do you suppose you will find in me your ideal?
Do you think it so easy to have me become your
lover?"

After hearing crap like that from Alan's mouth, I plugged out on the rest, turning my copy of it over to the blank side.

———

EVEN THOUGH I HAD A DRIVER'S LICENSE, I DIDN'T HAVE A WHIP of my own yet. So that same day, after football practice, I caught a ride home with Ethan. And as we pulled up in front of my house and saw all the cars parked in the driveway, I recognized Melody's metallic blue Cavalier right away.

"Your sis throwing a party or something?" Ethan asked.

"Must be the girls in that Fashion Club," I answered. "The ones on the bleachers from yesterday."

"Adonis, invite me in," Ethan said, combing his hair in the rearview mirror. "I'm up for a babe-mingle."

"All sweaty like this?" I said, and sniffed at my pits where I'd cut the sleeves off a T-shirt. "The two of us reek."

"Believe it or not, that musky scent gets girls going. It's all subconscious, ignites their hormones. I read about it in one of those men's health magazines."

"Are you sure?" I asked, taking a second sniff.

"Yeah, I'm sure. Sex isn't personal. It's all chemistry," Ethan said. "You just need to mix the right formula."

"Okay, but remember, Melody's mine."

"There's plenty to go around. I'm not going to plant my flag on your turf," Ethan assured me. "Not in your own house."

"I may need you to run interference for me and talk to whoever's near her, so I can get some one-on-one time. The same way I block those D-linemen for you to make a pass on the field."

"I got *your* back today, bro. But if she's surrounded by dog meat it's not happening. Hey, what if she's sitting on the couch next to your mom, looking at junior-high photos of your pudgy ass wearing braces?"

"It couldn't get any worse than that. Just tackle me on the stop," I answered, slamming the car door behind me and hauling my helmet by the face mask with my shoulder pads sitting snug on top of it.

I opened the front door and found the living room full of Jeannie's friends, talking and looking at fashion magazines in three or four different circles.

Barclay was hyped over all that company, and when me and Ethan walked inside, he began barking. Then he raced up to Ethan and started sniffing at his crotch. And he wouldn't stop, no matter how many times Ethan shoved him away.

"Come on, Barclay boy. Quit it," said Ethan, with most of the girls laughing hysterically over it.

"Barclay, down!" I ordered without any success.

I could see the embarrassment on Ethan's face right before he asked, "Adonis, since when did your dog turn homo?"

That's when all the laughing stopped, and I noticed Alan was part of the crowd.

"Ethan, honey, we don't use that kind of hateful language in this house," said Mom, who was in the living room, too.

"Yes, ma'am," said Ethan in an overly polite voice. "I apologize."

Melody was looking right at me. So I nodded to her with an approving smile, like Mom had handled Ethan perfectly.

Then Alan walked to the middle of the living room and cleared his throat.

"Miss Vice President, I think we've accomplished our agenda here of trying to organize our first fashion show, and more," Alan announced, looking at my sister. "Thanks to you and your family for letting us meet in your lovely home."

"Thank you all for coming," Jeannie said through a round of applause.

I made my way over to Melody and we'd just started talking when Ethan came up on one side of me, and Jeannie and Alan on the other.

There were no introductions between Alan and Ethan, and that was probably best.

"I'm out the door," Ethan said into my left ear, still fending off the dog.

"I hear you," I told him, grabbing Barclay by the collar before I turned back to Melody and said, "Hey, that's a really nice perfume you've got on."

"Oh, I'm not wearing any," she responded.

"That's Alan's perfume," said Jeannie with a wide grin.

"Yes, I was all perspired from gym and your darling

sister lent me a dash of fragrance to cover up. Do you really like it on me, Adonis?"

At that moment, I felt like I was a tightrope walker. That I was on a thin rope stretched a thousand feet up in the air over a bottomless pit with the wind pushing at me hard from every direction—with Melody and Ethan judging my every move.

And all I knew for sure was that I wasn't about to look down.

"I guess so," I answered, cautious, barely moving a muscle.

"Well, Adonis, I just wanted to thank you, too. I know you're coming home tired from football. It's an imposition to have visitors, and you must want to relax. But I can't wait to discuss those sports teams with you in English," said Alan.

Then Ethan slapped me on the back, and I swore I was going to fall.

"Like I said, I'm outta here, bro."

I steadied myself, catching my balance, like I really was up on that tightrope. And I slowly put one foot in front of the other as I walked Melody to her car.

"You know, you keep surprising me, Adonis," she said when we were finally alone outside. "I thought that perfume conversation would have made you, umm, *uncomfortable.*"

"Why? It's just different people, and different situations," I said with a straight face. "Everyone's not the same. So I'm accepting it. It's all I can do."

"Well, I was very impressed," she said, softly brushing her hair back to one side with her hand. "Hey, I know you're probably busy with practice and other stuff, but do you want to hang out this weekend?"

"Sure. I'll call you," I answered, trying not to show any excitement.

"Great. I look forward to it."

I could barely take my eyes off her round, plump lips. But I didn't go there, and I played it ultracool by giving her a little kiss good-bye, high on the cheek.

IT WAS NEARLY TEN O'CLOCK THAT NIGHT WHEN DAD GOT HOME from his shift. I was up in my room trying to learn how to jump rope, because the offensive-line coach said it would make me lighter on my feet. But I couldn't make more than two jumps in a row without getting tangled up, and my feet kept landing flat on the floor like an earthquake.

When Mom and Dad came upstairs for bed, they stopped at my open door.

"Son, I hear you're complimenting men on how they smell now," said Dad with a grin. "That's quite a change from your attitude yesterday."

"He's doing an English project with Alan, too," added Mom.

That's when Jeannie came out of her room and mocked, "Oh, yeah, I'm sure Adonis *volunteered* to work with him. Alan knows *so* much about sports."

"Hey, I can deal with it. And I never looked so good in front of Melody because of *him*."

"That's it, son. If you gotta put up with these types, use 'em to your best advantage."

"That's not tolerance," lectured Mom.

"What are you talking about? I'm *Mr. Tolerance*,"

Dad said, annoyed. "When everybody down at the firehouse figured that rookie for a fruit, I was the one who told the guys not to press him on it. That as long as he didn't talk about his boyfriend or his lifestyle in front of us, it was the same as if it wasn't true."

"And how fast did he put in for a transfer? Three weeks, was it?" asked Mom.

"That's because *he* was uncomfortable, not *me*," Dad defended himself.

"Adonis, tell me you were happy to see Alan in this house," Jeannie snapped from the hall.

"Hey, he's the president of your precious club. How come you didn't all go to *his* place?" I shot back, before I cleared the rope three times.

"Because his father doesn't approve. All right?" said Jeannie, stepping inside my room.

"See, I told you I was tolerant," crowed Dad.

"Just answer the question, Adonis," said Jeannie. "You don't want Alan here, do you?"

"If I say that, is it going to change him ever being here again?" I asked.

"No, it's not," Mom said, firm.

"Then why should I come off looking like a pig?"

"That's right, son," said Dad. "You're learning how to survive in this mixed-up world. I'm proud of you."

3

I saw Ethan sitting with some of our teammates in the school cafeteria, Godfrey, Bishop, Marshall, and Toby among them. Ethan wasn't much on passing up a good joke, especially at someone else's expense. So I held my breath over whether he was going to talk up that embarrassing scene at my house from the day before.

I'd known Ethan since the seventh grade, when I first went out for CYO football. Back then, I was an overweight kid looking for a position to play. Ethan was always a quarterback, and a leader. And he'd get lots of laughs by ranking on anybody new or different. In the beginning of our friendship, I'd heard it a few times from him about my weight.

He'd call me, "Aroundis," "Pudge," or "the Walking Buffet."

But those kinds of comments quit once I started blocking for him, when I made the varsity squad in my sophomore year.

Ethan's put-downs could be pretty rough to take. But sometimes they were funny, too.

Two years ago, in homeroom, D'Antoni called Ethan a "xenophobe," after he made a remark about the red dot on some Indian kid's forehead looking like the target from a laser scope on high-powered rifle.

"What are you talking about?" replied Ethan. "I don't play the xylophone. I'm not in the marching band. I'm a football player. And if I was in the band I'd play something manly, like the tuba."

Then D'Antoni explained that a xenophobe was someone who had a natural fear of strangers or people with different cultures.

"No offense, Mr. D," said Ethan, turning it back around on him. "But if that were true, and I was really one of those *phobes*, I would have transferred out of *your* homeroom after the first day."

D'Antoni responded with a long, cold stare, before he said, "I suppose it's good that students and *teachers* don't have that option, or else we'd never really get to know one another."

So with all that, I was surprised when Ethan didn't use yesterday's scene with Alan for a few laughs.

"Here's Adonis, the rock of our offensive line," Ethan said, punching me in the arm as I passed by with my tray.

"Just trying to carry my weight," I said, feeling relieved. "Same as always."

There weren't any open seats, and I hovered there for a few seconds. I was waiting for those guys to scoot their chairs closer together, so I could bring one over from another table. Only nobody did. I left to chow down with a group of juniors on the team instead. And I worried that a little bit of my status with Ethan and the other senior players was slipping away, all because of Alan.

At football practice that afternoon, the coaches pushed us hard, running through almost every formation in our playbook. I was really focused on my blocking and protection assignments, knocking a couple of defenders flat.

I thought it was my imagination that guys were slapping me congratulations on my backside more than usual, saying things like, "You smelled that one out," and "Adonis has got a real nose for the game."

Then, inside our last huddle, Ethan pulled us around him to bark out the play.

"Seventy-six queer, on two," he said, clapping his hands together to break us apart.

I stood there lost for a second, until I realized we had no such play.

Seventy-six was my number, and the other ten guys on offense were all staring straight at me.

"Yo, Adonis, how you like the smell of *our* perfume?" asked Bishop.

Then the bunch of them turned around, sticking their asses out at me to fart.

Five or six of those dudes ripped off good ones. And the stink hit me all at once. They were laughing themselves silly, with some of them rolling around on the ground, as the whistle blew to end practice.

I was laughing, too, but deep down it felt anything but funny.

"It matches your personalities, that perfume," I told them. "It really does. They ought to bottle it under the name 'Stink in the City.'"

Inside the locker room, Ethan was the first one to put his arm around me.

"Don't take it personal, Adonis," Ethan said with the rest of those guys listening. "You're still our boy. But I'm team captain. It's my job to keep us all loose. Somebody has to pay the price for that. Today it was you."

"Once we heard that story about you and gay boy's perfume, and they served baked beans today in the cafeteria, whew, it was on," explained Godfrey.

"You don't need to worry about me. I can take it," I said, twisting a damp towel tight. "But can you?"

I snapped that towel at Godfrey's rear end, and there was nothing but hooting and hollering in that locker room as I chased after him, and then the rest of them, with it.

After we'd changed, Ethan gave me another lift home. Only this time, Godfrey and Bishop were along for the ride.

I lived just four blocks from school, so I was riding shotgun, ready to get dropped off first.

I'd planned on buying a car before school started. But I only had enough savings from my summer job to get an old wreck. The truth was, I didn't want to be seen driving around town in one. Honestly, I couldn't afford to. I wasn't some big dork carrying a few extra pounds anymore.

I had an image.

I was a varsity football player—a starter. And I wasn't about to go backward in my life.

My parents, especially Mom, were worried about how safe I was going to be driving a clunker. They promised to buy me a *good* used car for my eighteenth birthday in December. So I decided I could hold out till then, with Mom letting me use her car most weekends in exchange for taking more responsibilities around the house, like hauling groceries and taking Jeannie places.

Right before we turned the last corner to my house, I started to stress thinking Alan might be there, sitting on the front steps with Jeannie. Then I imagined crazy things, like Alan would be holding hands with some other guy while he talked to her. That it would be something I'd never live down with my teammates.

I shut my eyes tight, and when I opened them again everything was normal outside my house. There were no extra cars in the driveway, no Fashion Club meeting—just Barclay sitting out front alone, barking and wagging his tail as we pulled up.

"What's Barclay, one of those border collies?" asked Bishop.

"I think he is," answered Godfrey, before I could say a word. "I hear they're supposed to be the smartest dog around, as smart as a monkey or a pig."

"A pig's smart?" said Ethan. "I don't think that's right."

"Yeah, pigs got big brains," said Godfrey. "Maybe they don't use 'em, rolling around in the mud all the time. But they got 'em. I seen one count to three with its foot, on TV."

"Well, he is a border collie, and that makes him pretty damn smart," I said as I opened the car door and Barclay jumped onto my lap.

"He looks happy to see you, Adonis," said Bishop.

"I think he's much happier to see Ethan," I said, holding Barclay back from trying to lick him. "His long-lost love."

But Godfrey and Bishop hadn't heard enough about yesterday to be laughing at Ethan over that.

And as I got out of the car with Barclay, I shot Ethan a look, knowing he'd only told the team half of yesterday's embarrassing shit. That he'd left out the part about Barclay's nose being buried in his crotch in front of all those girls.

"Adonis, you ought to get that dog *fixed*," cracked Ethan, backing his car out of the driveway.

"I didn't know he was broken," I said, patting Barclay on the head.

ON FRIDAY, I GOT TO MR. D'ANTONI'S ENGLISH CLASS WITH Toby and Marshall, just before the late bell.

Work on your projects today was written up on the green board in white chalk, and most of the chairs had been moved into groups.

"Cool, free period talking about sports," Toby said,

low. "How's your group going, Adonis? You know, with those three girls."

"I'll bet that fag tries to name your team the Fudge Packers," Marshall said even lower, with D'Antoni eyeing us from his desk.

"Not if I've got anything to do with it, he won't," I answered, starting toward my seat on the far side of the room.

Alan, Maxine, and Wendy were already sitting down, taking out their notes. But I hadn't done any research. I'd had a lifetime of watching and reading about sports, and all of the answers I needed were inside my head.

"Let's do this in an orderly fashion," D'Antoni told the class. "First, discuss the different teams already playing in your assigned cities. Then, talk about that city's history. Before the period's over, consider what sport *your* team might play and what names you might give it. Try to establish a list of both to work from. We'll worry about creating a logo down the line."

"So, what kind of information did our two sports

people dig up?" Alan asked me and Wendy, staring at my empty desktop.

"Baseball, Cincinnati Reds," I said with complete confidence. "Football, Cincinnati Bengals. College, it's the University of Cincinnati Bearcats. That's all of them. I knew it cold since I was a kid."

Maxine caught me off guard and asked, "What's a bearcat?"

"How should I know, there's probably no such thing," I said. "Bears and cats can't get it on. And nobody cares. Believe me, Cincinnati's all about the Bengals and the Reds."

Then Wendy looked down at her notes and said, "Well, actually the baseball team's real name is the Red Stockings. They were the first professional baseball team, established in eighteen sixty-nine."

"Oh, the Red Stockings, I like that," said Maxine, running her hand over the six different colored bracelets on her right wrist.

"I think I see how we can dress our new team. It's a natural," Alan said.

"Red Stockings?" asked Maxine.

"All the way up to the knee," answered Alan, smiling.

"They call them the Reds for short," I said, frustrated. "Nowadays, nobody says 'Red Stockings.' It's just 'Reds.' Read any newspaper, any sports section."

When Maxine and Alan started their part of the project, I took out a pen and a sheet of paper, just to be polite and to keep D'Antoni from getting on my back.

I scribbled down what Maxine said about Cincinnati being on the Ohio River, about all the steamboats that used to ride down that river, and how lots of soldiers from the Revolutionary War were given land there. Then she told us that Cincinnati is where they make Ivory Soap.

"It became world famous as 'the soap that floats,'" she said.

"Maybe we should call our team the Floaters," I joked. "Dress 'em in brown."

Wendy made a disgusted face, like I'd taken a dump on my desk, and Maxine said, "Ewww, that's gross."

I was shocked that Alan was laughing along with me.

"It *is* gross. But it's funny, too," he said. "You should consider a career in advertising or comedy writing, Adonis."

"Maybe I should," I said coy, staring straight at him. "Everything looks and sounds *funny* to me."

"You know, I've let a lot of your little remarks go because you're Jeannie's brother. But don't take advantage of that," said Alan, staring straight back at me.

Before I could respond, D'Antoni interrupted the class and said, "Let's hear a little bit from each group, so we have a feel for what's going on around us."

So I had to hold my tongue and listen to the history of nowhere places like Oklahoma City, Sacramento, and Boise. A girl in another group talked about Omaha, and Alan turned to us and mouthed, "I used to live in Omaha."

All I knew about Nebraska was that it was smack in the middle of the country, and that the college football team was called the Nebraska Cornhuskers. I could picture Alan and his gay Omaha friends sitting in a field eating corn on the cob.

When it was our group's turn, we agreed that Alan would speak.

He mentioned the steamboats, soldiers, and soap, and called the baseball team the "Red Stockings-slash-Reds."

Then Alan said, "Cincinnati is also called the Queen City."

I almost fell out of my seat when he said it.

Toby and a couple of other guys laughed out loud, and I swore I heard Marshall say "ho-mo" inside of clearing his throat.

"Quiet! Quiet down!" shouted D'Antoni, nearly losing his hippie temper.

"May I continue?" Alan asked. D'Antoni nodded to him. "It was called the Queen City because it had so much growth and prosperity. People were proud of it."

When Alan took a long pause, I thought he was finished. But he stood up, turned to look at Marshall, and said, "Now if *you* only had some growth, I mean more than just the hair on your upper lip, somebody might compliment you sometime."

Marshall shot to his feet. He almost had to. He couldn't let a fag like Alan disrespect him that way in public.

"You got something to say to *me?*" he challenged Alan with maybe ten feet separating them.

Me and Toby jumped up out of our chairs and got in front of Marshall.

"He's not worth it," Toby whispered to him. "Don't get kicked off the team over that mistake of nature."

Marshall had five inches and maybe seventy pounds of pure muscle on Alan.

It would have been like a horned rhino charging a feathered peacock if they'd fought. But Alan never flinched. He looked steady as anything, like nothing Marshall had said could shake him. And I couldn't tell if he was brave or just plain clueless.

Finally, Marshall came to his senses and sat back down, leaving Alan standing up alone.

"I won't tolerate this kind of aggressive behavior," said D'Antoni, who seemed as annoyed at Alan as he was at Marshall. "I'll see you both after class."

When we got back to working in our groups, Alan said, "Thank you for calming down your friend, Adonis. I appreciate what you did."

"Yeah, yeah," I said, trying to brush him off. "Just don't expect me to make a habit of it."

Maxine changed the subject, asking Alan, "So you lived in Omaha?"

"Two years ago, for almost a full semester," he said. "That was right after my grandmother died, and I started living with my father. He works for the military, traveling from base to base. So I've gone to high school in, let's see, Spokane, Houston, Indianapolis, Omaha, and oh, yes, here. Go Wildcats!"

"It must be hard to pick up and move like that all the time," said Wendy.

"I really have felt like Peter Pan flying all over the place, living in Neverland. Only my Captain Hook's an army colonel, and every morning it's 'Yes, sir,'" said Alan, snapping off a mock salute from beneath his blond bangs. "But he's got a stable job in recruiting now, so I should finish out my senior year in one place. Anyway, the military's what gave me my love of fashion. Those dress blue uniforms, button-down navy peacoats, and the leather bomber jackets with the fur collars—that's style."

"You must miss your grandmother a lot," said Maxine.

"I do. She was everything to me," said Alan. "She was a tough lady who taught me how to take care of myself. She'd say, 'Alan, you can walk away, step aside, or fight if you have to. But never stoop down lower than the troublemaker in front of you.' I hear those words of hers in my mind every day."

"That's your father's mom?" Maxine asked.

"Yes. She raised five of her own daughters, my father, and me," answered Alan. "And the only one of them who didn't learn to communicate happens to be my *superior officer*."

"What about your mother?" asked Wendy. "Where's she?"

"She's not around anymore. I don't talk much about her," he answered.

"I respect that," said Wendy, with Maxine nodding her head in agreement.

Right then, I wished I could have pulled out the world's smallest violin to play behind them.

"By the way, Adonis," Alan said, "I almost forgot—Cincinnati was the first city in America to have a full-time fire department. Your father's a fireman, isn't he?"

"Yup,"

"Did you ever live anywhere else?" he asked me.

"Nope. One house. Two schools."

"Must be why you're so straightforward," he said. "It's a good quality to always say what you're thinking."

I just shrugged my shoulders, hoping to put an end to that one-way conversation.

Maxine said, "I'm thinking our team should be a gymnastics squad."

"But that doesn't draw big crowds," said Wendy. "How about this—it's cold in Cincinnati in the winter, and they don't have a hockey team."

I reached over and grabbed the sheet of notes from

Alan's desk. At the bottom of it I wrote FOOTBALL in capital letters.

"That's what excites a city," I said, tapping the paper with my pen. "Football. Hard hitting, smash-mouth football. Not balance beams and Zambonis."

"Zam-*what*?" asked Alan with his question getting Toby's attention from the next group over.

But I wouldn't answer. I didn't want the guys getting the wrong idea, seeing me talking so much to Alan.

"Zamboni. It smoothes out the ice," Maxine said. "I know that from figure skating."

In the end, we hadn't settled on a sport yet, but we came up with four possible names—the Steamers, for the steamboats; the Revs, for the Revolutionary War soldiers; the Monarchs, for Cincinnati being called the Queen City; and the Blaze, for having the first fire department.

After the bell rang and I'd packed up, I stopped at the door with Toby.

I looked back at Marshall and Alan standing on either side of D'Antoni's desk, getting read the riot act.

I'd always admired Marshall because he wouldn't

back down from anybody, no matter how big or tough, on the football field or anywhere else. I guess Alan had just done the same thing in challenging Marshall. But I wouldn't think of giving him one-tenth of that respect.

I wasn't ready to cross that kind of line.

4

That night was my date with Melody, our third official one. And after football practice, when the guys were talking about their plans for the weekend, I found a way to let it slip that this time *she'd* asked *me* out. Of course, I didn't mention it had anything to do with the way Melody thought I'd handled that remark about Alan's perfume.

"I'm taking her to that retro drive-in movie theater, over in Park Heights," I told them. "That'll give us some built-in privacy. Sit in the car, tune the radio in to the movie soundtrack, a little chill in the night, huddle together for some warmth—I think I got the right play called on this one."

"Third date, her idea—better bring some protection," said Bishop. "How big's the backseat of your mother's car?"

"Don't even sound right. Being with a female in the backseat of your *mother's* car," said Godfrey. "What about your pop's Firebird, the hot Trans Am?"

"Tell 'em, Adonis," said Ethan. "Tell 'em why your pop won't let you borrow his classic wheels anymore."

I was just happy that Ethan was moving off of me as the punch line to any kind of joke, even if it did jab at Dad.

"Because he got an emergency call from his job one time while I was out driving it," I said. "My mom was out with her car, too, so he had to wait for a cab."

"Now, tell 'em where the fire was," said Ethan, cracking himself up.

"In his own firehouse," I said, fighting back a grin. "And in English that week, we'd been studying irony. So I used it as an example on the exam—part of the firehouse burned down because the firemen weren't there. I aced it and hung the paper up on our fridge. He walked past it every day for a week saying, 'My son the genius.' Then one day he actually read it and freaked out on me."

Guys who hadn't heard that story before loved it, and I walked off with them laughing their asses off.

"Tell those dudes over in Park Heights we're going to score all over them in the game next week," Bishop called after me. "Let them know you came up there to *score* with your girl first, to get in the mood."

I wasn't sure about all of that. But I'd planned on carrying a condom inside my wallet anyway.

Melody dated a lot, mostly preppy-intellectual types. I had no clue how far she'd gone with anybody else. I just knew we weren't exclusive or anything, and she really wasn't mine. And I figured good-looking guys with hot sports cars were probably hitting on her every day, especially after seeing she'd go out with half-a-pudge like me.

Later on, at home, I stepped out of a long, hot shower and wiped the steam off the bathroom mirror. I tightened my abs as much as I could. Then I lifted my arms and flexed my biceps a few times.

I almost liked what I saw.

All that extra weight lifting was starting to pay off, and I could see some more muscle definition. But I was still too soft in lots of places.

I lathered up my face, and when I finished with the razor, I splashed on some of Dad's aftershave. Then I winced, as I fought off the sting to my open pores.

"You smell nice," Mom said after I'd dressed and gone downstairs.

She was sitting in the living room with Jeannie, watching the end of some sappy chick-flick on cable they'd probably seen a dozen times. They both had bowls in their laps and were having soup for supper.

Dad was working that night, so we didn't stick to our six thirty family-dinner rule.

"Is that Dad's aftershave?" Jeannie asked. "Because I was thinking how that's the same as perfume."

"It's made for *men*, like cologne," I said. "Nice try."

"Just has a different name," said Jeannie between spoonfuls of soup. "For marketing purposes."

"I think everyone has a masculine and feminine side," Mom said. "It's nothing to be ashamed of."

"Well, I don't."

"Are you sure? You used to play with dolls all the time," said Jeannie.

"When?"

"When you were little. Remember the G.I. Joe, Hulk Hogan, and all those wrestler dolls I bought you?" said Mom.

"You know, the ones with the cute little shorts and all those rippling muscles," added Jeannie. "They were so gorgeous."

"*Dolls?* Those were action figures. They had guns and grenades, or they beat the crap out of each other."

"If that's what you want to believe," said Jeannie, smirking.

"All right, Jeannie. Let's not do this to your brother as he's walking out the door on a date. We shouldn't give him a complex right now."

"Poor Melody won't know who she's out with—a football stud or a doll collector," said Jeannie.

"You're a million laughs. And what are you doing tonight?"

"A bunch of us are hanging out together—guys and girls."

"Yeah, I just bet one of those guys is really half girl."

"Adonis, I told you that's unacceptable," chided Mom, rattling a spoon against the side of her soup bowl.

"At least Alan doesn't hide his feminine side," said Jeannie. "Not like a team of butt-slapping, crotch-grabbing football players who shower together."

I let that remark go, and then went into the kitchen where I made myself a ham sandwich. I even dropped a slice into Barclay's dish for him to find later.

Wolfing that sandwich down, I thought about how Godfrey said a pig was so smart. Only not smart enough to avoid becoming our dinner.

By ten minutes to seven, I was out the door to pick up Melody.

Before I drove off, I looked over the backseat of Mom's Honda.

I shoved the seat belts and metal buckles down beneath the cushions. Then I stashed the Public Television tote bag and umbrella inside the trunk.

In the front, I thought hard about taking the plastic statue of Jesus off the dashboard and slipping it into the glove compartment. But I stressed that Melody might have remembered it being there, or I'd forget to put it back for Mom. Then I'd have to come up with a reason for taking it down. So I decided to leave it.

When I got to Melody's house, I popped a breath mint and walked up to the front door. She opened it before I ever rang the bell. That's when I found out that she wanted to change our plans.

"It turns out my parents are at a party tonight. We've got the place to ourselves. Instead of going to a movie, want to hang out here?" she asked with a flirty smile that nearly made my knees buckle.

"Sure, that's great," I said with every bell and whistle going off inside my head, thinking she wanted me bad. "Your parents won't care that you've got a guy in the house?"

"No, they trust me and my judgment."

I never saw Melody look so sexy. She was wearing tight jeans and a silky red blouse with a neckline that plunged low enough to hold my attention there.

I circled the living room, looking at pictures of Melody and her family. Then I tried to act suave and ran a finger across the keys on their piano—*brrrrrrrrrpt.*

Finally, I sat down on the couch. But Melody parked herself on one side of a small table with a chess set on top of it.

"You know how to play?" she asked.

I was pretty disappointed. I'd heard of strip poker but never of anybody playing strip chess.

"A little bit," I answered, getting up and taking the seat across from her. "Ladies first."

"No, the white always goes first. That's you."

I moved one of my pawns up two spaces, like Dad had taught me to open the game. Then Melody did the same with her pawn opposite mine, to block me from advancing any farther.

"So, do you know what you're doing for college next year?" she asked.

"I definitely want to go. But I'm not sure where, or what I'd study. How 'bout you?"

"I want to study design somewhere, maybe at State. That's why I joined the Fashion Club, to see the work of different designers, get new perspectives."

"You mean it's more than just the hot clothes for

you," I said with a sly smile, moving another piece forward.

"Yes, it is," she said, grinning. "I figured you wanted to study mechanics. You seemed so into cars when I first met you."

"Oh, the service station? That was just a job. I mean, I like cars a lot. But I don't know about mechanics in college."

"It's not a real passion for you, huh?"

"No, not like football."

"Really, what turns you on about it?"

I couldn't believe it, but I actually had to think for a few seconds before I could give her an answer.

"Well, I guess it's being part of the team, knowing we're all together and working for the same thing—to win."

"I've noticed at games you don't get to run with the ball. How come?"

"I'm just a blocker, for whoever's carrying the pigskin. That's what I do best. I know it's not glamorous or anything. It's more like grunt work. But it's really important. Without good blocking, the ball carrier would get creamed on every play."

"Oh, I get it. So that's why the blockers don't get treated like heroes, right? Because they're not scoring the touchdowns. That's totally unfair."

"I figure if I was meant to be a hero I would be," I said. "I have this dream, though, that Ethan or one of the other guys fumbles. I pick up the ball and dodge tackler after tackler, running it in for a touchdown. I've even got this little celebration dance planned out in my head."

"Do it for me, the dance."

"No, I can't. It's too silly."

"Please, I want to see it," she said, coming around to pull out my chair.

With all that talk about what turns me on and wanting to see me dance, I couldn't tell if she was making a move on me or not.

I stood up, self-conscious as anything.

"All right. Here it is," I said, deciding to go for it.

First, I raised my arm and spiked an imaginary

football. Then I marched in a small circle, like a drum major leading the band.

"Go, Adonis!" Melody shouted, cheering me on.

Hearing that gave me the confidence to put my hands on my knees, shuffling them back and forth, like my legs could pass through each other. I finished by pulling two invisible six-guns from holsters on my hips and shooting them off into the air.

"That was great," she said, clapping. "I hope you get to do that dance for real one day, and I'm there to see it."

Then Melody gave me a deep, wet kiss, and part of me felt like I really had just crossed the goal line and scored a touchdown.

When we sat back down, I looked at the chessboard and realized I already had nowhere to move without surrendering my strongest pieces.

"You know what," Melody said, getting up. "There's another game upstairs. One I haven't played for a long time."

My ears perked up at hearing that. I thought she was asking me to go up to her bedroom with her, and I could feel my heart start to race.

But then she took off fast up the stairs alone. It didn't seem like I was supposed to follow her, even though I wanted to. I stood there alone for almost a minute. And I went back and forth in my head a few times, until I decided I needed to make a move.

But when I got to the stairs, Melody was already on her way back down holding a pair of Rock 'Em Sock 'Em Robots.

"This is my brother's. I used to play with him all the time, before he left for college," she said, excited. "I'm guessing you know how?"

"Bring it on," I answered, feeling stupid on the inside for thinking she couldn't resist me.

We cleared the chess set from the table. Then I took the red robot and she had the blue. Melody was pretty good.

"I knocked your block off, Adonis!" she shouted, the first time her robot beat mine.

But my robot won eight of the twelve rounds we fought, and I guess that made up for getting my ass whipped at chess.

After that, we played darts outside on her patio,

and then watched a little TV with our hands clasped together.

The whole time I was at her house, Melody was as much a friend as she was a date. I didn't expect that when I walked through the door. But it was all right. And in the end, it took a lot of pressure off me, instead of worrying over when to make my big move.

By nine thirty, I was driving us over to Johnny Rockets, a local burger place and hangout inside the Tri-County Mall, about a mile from Central High. Rockets is on the first floor, sandwiched between a Gap and Victoria's Secret. Its rear exit opens up onto the inner concourse, where you can sit on the benches by the indoor trees and water fountains, and where the TC Mall sometimes has free entertainment, like jugglers, magicians, and wannabe pop stars.

Inside the place, an old-fashioned jukebox was blaring music. I was steering us across the checkered floor, toward an open table, when Melody said, "Hey, there's your sister, with some people from the Fashion Club. Let's stop for a second and say hi."

I changed direction without saying a word. But it was the last thing I wanted to do.

Jeannie was sitting with Alan, Maxine, and another girl.

"Here's the best-smelling football player I know," said Jeannie as we got within a few feet.

"Oh, I want to ask these two what we were talking about before," Alan said. "Did you ever notice that when you're part of a group of boys and girls, someone could say, 'Come on, *guys*, let's go do this or that,' but you can never say, 'Come on, *girls*,' to a mixed group?"

"I guess I never thought about it like that before," said Melody.

"Right? Neither did I," said Maxine, with a pair of purple sunglasses sitting on top of her head. "It's the way women get shortchanged in the language."

I just nodded my head and glanced around at the surrounding tables to see who else might have been listening. But everyone seemed to be into their own conversations.

"Well, we'd ask you to join us, but you probably want your privacy," said Alan.

"Yeah, we do," I said, taking Melody's hand to leave. "Sis, I'll see you at home."

That table I'd first spotted was filled now, so we started toward an open one way in the back.

"Hey, Adonis," Ethan called out.

He was sitting at a long table with some of our teammates and their girlfriends, mostly cheerleaders.

Melody moved in that direction with me, but I could feel the little bit of resistance in her.

"What you been up to tonight?" Ethan asked, with his girlfriend practically sitting on his lap. "Ever catch that drive-in flick?"

"No, we had something better than a movie on the agenda," I answered, pulling Melody in closer. "More personal."

Then I gave Ethan a little wink that Melody never saw.

He grinned back at me, and I knew he'd take it to mean I'd scored.

"Way to go," he said, before he gave his girlfriend a long, openmouthed kiss.

I could feel there wasn't much warmth between

Melody and the cheerleaders. And I figured it was one of those territorial girl things.

That's when Melody tugged at my arm to leave, and I told them all, "Later."

When we got to our table, Melody said, "That's so gross. If they had some privacy, fine. But do we really need a front-row seat to watch him stick his tongue down her throat? What's he trying to prove?"

"I agree with you," I said. "It's just a show."

"No offense, I know he's your friend and all. But I'm glad you don't think like him, with that kind of jock mentality."

"No. No. You're right. Absolutely."

"You know, that's part of what I like about you, Adonis. You're so yourself, such a contradiction from those guys. You can play football with them but still be who *you* want to be. I think that's really cool."

"I think the same way about you. That you don't have to act the way some of those cheerleaders do to get attention. You can play Rock 'Em Sock 'Em Robots on a date and still be a good time."

"That's very sweet," she said, grabbing my hand and squeezing it inside of hers.

After hearing that description of her out of my own mouth, I felt terrible about the way I'd played Melody in front of Ethan. But if I had to do it over, I'd have probably done it the same.

5

Early Saturday afternoon, I jogged over to the weight room at the edge of the athletic field. I even did a few slow laps on the running track with that damn jump rope dangling around my neck when I first got there.

A dozen of my teammates were inside doing extra training, including Marshall and Toby, and we took turns lifting and spotting for each other.

"How you doing with the stupid jump rope?" Marshall asked me between sets of bench presses. "You ready to hang yourself with it yet?"

"I can make threesies," I answered, laughing at myself.

"That's about where I am, man," said Marshall.

Then Toby grabbed the rope and said, "Watch this. I can keep it going good."

He jumped twelve times in a row. Only he did it like a caveman, pounding each one out, without any rhythm at all.

"That's not what Coach meant about us getting lighter on our feet," I said. "He wants us to change our approach."

"I think Coach forgot who we are. Maybe he should get that *Alana* to teach us," said Marshall, swinging his wrists in two small circles and skipping an invisible rope. "Queer boy can sing, '*Strawberry shortcake cream on top.*'"

"I'm so glad you didn't wipe the floor with him in English," I said. "They would have suspended you from school *and* the team."

"Adonis, did we tell you? We're going to meet that dude's pops later," Toby said. "Right after this."

"What do you mean?" I asked.

"You know my cousin Gavin. Well, he went to that big military recruiting office downtown. The one with all the branches together—army, navy, air force, marines," Marshall said. "The head officer over there is queer boy's father—the colonel. My cousin saw that his name tag said HARPRING. So he asked him, 'Do you have a relative that goes to my high school, Alan Harpring?' 'That's my son,' he says. 'But you won't be in any competition with him for a good assignment in the military. He's not the type.'"

"Imagine your own pops doing you like that to a stranger," said Toby.

"Makes sense to me," said Marshall. "A colonel's not some nobody private or corporal. He's got a serious rep to uphold."

Even so, I couldn't imagine Dad dumping on me that way, no matter how much I disappointed him.

For months, Toby and Marshall had been talking about joining the military.

I thought that fit them perfectly.

Toby seemed to like taking orders. And Marshall, who already had a buzz cut, was good at giving them, unless Ethan was barking them out. Then they were both good soldiers, usually following through on whatever Ethan said.

Maybe I was in that army, too. But at least I could think for myself and make my own decisions.

I hadn't given much thought to joining the real military.

Dad had served five years in the Coast Guard Reserves. He'd always said it helped him land the job with the fire department. So when those two offered me a ride to the recruiting office with them, I decided to tag along and check it out. But deep down, I was probably more interested in seeing what Alan's father was like.

We walked into the recruiting office, past all the posters of straight-backed steel-eyed men in uniforms that read, BE ALL YOU CAN BE; AN ARMY OF ONE; CROSS INTO THE BLUE; and THE FEW, THE PROUD.

A sergeant told us the high-school recruits were at a park two blocks away, doing physical training.

"They're all high-school students like yourselves, interested in the military way of life, and what wearing a uniform can bring them," said the sergeant. "Some are waiting till they graduate to sign up. Others are testing it out, making sure it's a commitment they want to make. Either way, you'll have to speak with Colonel Harpring first, and that's where he is, grooming the recruits."

The three of us were wearing sweats, so when we arrived at the park, Alan's father must have figured we belonged to that group of high-school recruits. There were nearly twenty of them doing jumping jacks, with him watching through a pair of dark shades.

"Soldiers are never late," he snapped at us. "That's because we're not individuals. We arrive, train, and leave together as a unit. I've already stressed this to you."

"No, sir," Toby said. "We've never met you before. This is our first time here."

Colonel Harpring was a half inch taller than me—or maybe he just stood up straighter. His barrel chest was decorated with at least ten shining medals, topped off by a silver eagle looking off to the side. And despite standing in the bright sun in his uniform jacket and hat, he was the only one of us who wasn't sweating.

"We came by to find out about joining up after we graduate," Marshall said. "We go to *Central High*, sir."

It sounded like Marshall said "Central High" fishing for a reaction from the colonel about Alan. But there wasn't any.

Instead, the colonel arched his back, took off his shades, and said, "We've had both successes and failures with recruits from Central before. However, whether you're a success or a failure is squarely on your own shoulders, no one else's."

I wasn't about to mention Alan's name. And I knew Marshall and Toby weren't really interested in getting on the wrong side of him, either.

"Compete at any team sports there?" he asked us. "That's the mark of a military mind-set."

"Varsity football," Marshall answered. "We're starters on the offensive line."

He asked our names, and when I told him, "Adonis," he said, "That's a strong name, full of character. Maybe you'll be one of the success stories. Perhaps that name will provide the backbone you'll need. How did you come by it?"

I skipped the part about that naked statue with the

perfect body, and I told him how Dad had named me after his favorite wrestler.

"Adrian Adonis," the colonel said. "I remember him well. A pretty boy with long, golden locks of hair. He was a beast of a man, but his vanity always got in the way. He lost a match one time looking for a mirror."

I went on to say how Dad served in the Coast Guard. But I could tell the colonel had stopped listening before I was finished.

"Join the others in some PT for now," he ordered. "PT, that's physical training—the body and mind working as one, a single weapon. We'll discuss your recruitment options later."

I put my nose down into the grass to do push-ups, thinking how it couldn't have been his father's fault that Alan was the way he was. The colonel looked solid as a rock and could have been the figure on any of those recruiting posters.

So I figured that maybe Alan's mother was one of those closet lesbians, passing down some kind of gay gene to him. And that's why she wasn't in the picture anymore.

PT ended when the sergeant from the recruiting office showed up in a camouflage-painted truck. Then all of those gung-ho high-school recruits, half of them with buzz cuts, started unloading chairs and fold-up tables from the back of it.

The sergeant set up trays of food filled with fried chicken, potato salad, and coleslaw.

"That's the best part of the military," said Marshall. "They feed you, give you clothes, and put a roof over your head—all for free. All you got to do is say 'Yes, *sir*,' and let them do the thinking for you."

No one touched a bite until everyone was seated and had a plate of food in front of them. There was one open seat at the head of the table, and I thought that was being saved for Alan's father. But the sergeant took it instead.

I asked Toby and Marshall about that, and Toby said, "Officers only eat with other officers. A colonel probably wouldn't even talk to recruits if it wasn't his job to get them to join up. He'd mostly tell a sergeant or somebody what he wanted, and they'd tell you."

On the sergeant's order, we all started to chow down. It was almost like having a picnic in the park with rules and regulations. And if an army of puny ants had shown up to ruin it, I'm sure we would have wiped them off the face of the earth.

Alan's father stood watching from about fifteen feet away while we ate, without saying a single word. He even had someone else hand the three of us recruiting folders with his name and phone number on them.

"He must want to disown his fag son," whispered Marshall.

"Big-time," said Toby. "Alan's the crud from his gene pool, real pond scum."

"What kinds of things do you think they do together?" I asked.

"I don't know," answered Marshall. "But I could make a whole list of the things they don't do."

"Yeah, like get facials and have their nails done," said Toby.

I figured Colonel Harpring was an expert at forcing recruits to fall into line for their own good. The same

way Dad had learned to hoist someone who was uncon-
scious onto his shoulders and carry him from a burning
building.

So Alan must have just been a hopeless case.

LATER THAT AFTERNOON, WHILE JEANNIE WAS DOING HER
homework at the kitchen table, I said, "I met your
friend's father, the colonel, down at the recruiting
office. Are you sure they're related? I've never seen two
more total opp—"

"I don't want to hear about it," Jeannie cut me off.
"What I know from Alan is that he's a bully, with lots
of problems about his own identity."

"Are you serious? His father's a big-shot officer down
there," I said, grabbing an almost-empty quart of milk
from the fridge, before lifting the carton to my lips.

"And why do you think he needs to be a big shot in
a uniform?" asked Jeannie. "Because he's confident or
insecure?"

I wiped my sleeve across my mouth and said, "That's
crazy talk. Who sold you on that? Alan? Because I don't

think identity is something he's got his arms wrapped completely around."

"Why don't you enlist with his father, then? You already wear one stupid uniform. What are you going to do for status when high school's over? You're not getting a football scholarship to college. None of you are. You only won three out of ten games last year."

"Get lost! And there's no status for you in being vice president of the Fashion Club?"

"Why would you ask that? You don't think there's any for Alan in being president," she said, tapping her pen on the open page in front of her.

"Hey, even if me and my teammates do lose games, at least we know what we are—*straight*."

Once that came out of my mouth, I knew it sounded way too mean. But she was the one who'd started it.

"And who did you go to the recruiting office with?"

"Toby and Marshall."

"So the three of you were just checking out joining a *new team*. One where you'll sleep in a barrack full of men, with no women around. Maybe you and your friends should look a little closer at yourselves, Adonis."

"And it's not the same in the Fashion Club when girls try to dress each other to look hot?"

"Then I guess you just proved it. Alan's the only straight one here," said Jeannie, slamming her notebook shut.

I had more I could say, but I didn't want to go another round with her. So I bit my tongue, and I let Jeannie collect all her books and walk off thinking she'd won something.

I stayed home that night to do my own schoolwork and study my playbook.

Dad was on duty at the firehouse, so Mom called out the plays for me. I listened to the numbers and told her where I was supposed to be on the field.

"Pro right, fifteen smash," said Mom.

"Fifteen is Ethan's number. That's a quarterback sneak," I said. "I don't go anywhere. I just get as low and strong as I can, and try to move the pile of players at the line of scrimmage forward."

After my nailing thirty of them in a row, Mom asked, "How come you can memorize all of these numbers and symbols, but you can't pull an A in trigonometry?"

The answer was because it didn't mean as much to me as football.

But I was smart enough to just shrug my shoulders and say, "I just can't figure it out. I must have some kind of mental block."

Then Mom asked out of nowhere, "How'd your date with Melody go?"

My brain froze for a second, searching for the right story. Until I realized I could tell Mom the truth, because nothing had really happened.

"Her parents were at a party, so we hung out at her house and played games."

"*Games*, huh? Well, you must have had your fill of fun then, to be staying home on a Saturday night."

"No, really, we played games. And I don't mean Truth or Dare. We played board games and stuff," I said. "I'm just tired tonight. I had two training sessions today, with some of my teammates in the morning and those recruits in the afternoon."

"Yeah, I've heard enough about the idea of you in the military for a while. I'm still getting used to the violence of football. I don't need to think about you being in a war zone somewhere," said Mom as she handed me back my playbook.

"That's all right, I'm not sold on it, either."

Another part of staying home that night had to do with me not wanting to run into Melody. She could be out with her friends, and I didn't want to stress over saying or doing the right things if I ran into her.

I left everything perfect with Melody last night, asking her out for next Saturday at the end of our date. I'd lined it up great, knowing she'd be in the stands for our home game next Friday under the lights. And I'd probably see her after the game, too, while I was still in my uniform. So it was going to be like having a lock on her for most of the weekend.

Before I went to bed, the sweet smell of chocolate filled the house.

It wasn't easy, but I passed on the walnut brownies Mom and Jeannie baked.

"I'm in serious training!" I called down to them from my bedroom. "Don't tempt me!"

I looked into the mirror and pinched more than an inch of blubber around my belly. Then I thought about how I might look in swim trunks next summer, standing beside Melody in a bikini.

So I got down on the floor, hoping to knock out two hundred crunches.

I almost made it, but I started to really sweat. And Barclay tried licking at my face so hard, I had to quit with thirty left to go.

ON SUNDAY AFTERNOON, DAD WAS HOME AND WE BOTH SET-tled on the living room couch to watch the opening week of pro football on TV. The Baltimore Ravens were playing the Washington Redskins in the first game.

"I guess for the next five months, until the Super Bowl, you two are going to dedicate nine hours of every Sunday to parking yourselves in front of that TV and watching football—the one o'clock game, the four o'clock game, the Sunday night game. Oh, and I forgot, Monday Night Football," said Mom, who was sitting at a side table making her third-grade lesson plans for the following week. "I tell my students all the time, 'Forget the video games and SpongeBob cartoons—go out and play, get some exercise.' Don't you two ever feel like you're wasting your lives, watching other people live theirs?"

"Excuse me, that's why I actually *play* football," I answered.

"And what's your excuse?" she asked Dad.

"In case you've forgotten, I *save* lives so people can live them," he said, dipping another chip into a bowl of salsa. "This is my relaxation, and it's time I spend with my son."

"Besides, it's educational, too," I told Mom. "Do you know how the Ravens got their name?"

"Tell me," she said. "I can't wait to hear."

"It's from that poem 'The Raven.' The writer's buried in Baltimore."

"Is that why their uniforms are purple, because of Poe's purple curtains?" she asked.

"What curtains?" I said, confused.

"The ones in the poem you've obviously never read," she said.

"I read it once—*Nevermore*," I said with a grin.

Dad even gave me a high five over that line.

"Do you know lots of Native Americans consider the name 'Redskins' to be an insult and a slur?" Mom asked. "There are even some newspapers that won't print their name, and just call them 'Washington.'"

"All nonsense," said Dad. "They should never change a team's name on account of that. It's tradition, what people are used to hearing."

"They say it's as insulting as if there was a team called the N-word after African Americans or the S-word after Hispanics," Mom kept on.

Then I turned to Dad and asked, "You've heard of the Green Bay Packers, right? Well, you know what my friend Marshall said Alan would want to name our project team in English class?"

"No, what?"

"The Fudge Packers."

"So that's the project you're working on with Alan," Mom said over Dad's laughing. "Now I get your Ravens comment."

"Know who'd be the most popular player on that Fudge Packers team?" Dad asked me.

"No, who?"

"Don't say it," Mom warned him.

"The tight end," said Dad as Mom picked up all of her books and headed for the kitchen.

"I'll leave you two *children* alone," she said, annoyed. "Let me know if either of you grows up anytime soon."

"Your mother doesn't understand what we share. That when it comes to fathers and sons, the apple doesn't fall far from the tree."

"You wouldn't know it by seeing Alan's dad, the colonel."

"That's exactly what I mean. He's got no reason to complain," Dad said, starting to crack up again. "From what you tell me, at least his son's some kind of *fruit*."

And we shared a double-handed high five to celebrate that one.

The game was going great, with lots of hard hitting. That had me and Dad pumped. So at halftime, we grabbed a football and went out into the backyard to have a catch. And we made a point to tell Mom that we were getting our butts outside for some exercise and to "live our own lives" for a while.

Dad could really throw a tight spiral, better than me.

I'd watch the spinning laces on the ball cut through the air and into my hands.

Barclay ran back and forth between us, shadowing the first twenty passes or so, before he hunkered down in the grass, exhausted.

"You serious at all about the military?" Dad asked. "It's a big commitment."

"I don't know. They ask an awful lot from you. Maybe the reserves."

"Not much different than being on a football team," Dad said, throwing me another bullet pass. "I've got confidence you could handle it."

"I hate to say it, but Alan's dad looked pretty impressive with all those medals pinned to his chest. That would turn girls' heads."

In my mind, I had a picture of Melody hanging off my arm, with me dressed in a sharp-creased military uniform.

"What was your rank in the Coast Guard Reserves?" I asked Dad.

"I was a seaman, first class."

"That's it? No medals or nothing?"

"Look, that colonel's a lifer. Probably took him a lot of years to move up the ranks. I had other talents. I was practically born to be a firefighter."

"How's that?"

"I can smell smoke a mile away."

I was about to say, *Yeah, as long as it's not in your own firehouse.*

But I didn't.

Dad's arm must have been getting tired, because his next pass missed me by five feet. And I had to chase it to the far corner of the yard, up against the back fence where Barclay usually did his business.

I could smell the stench of urine soaked into the ground when I picked up the ball, and I didn't want to even touch it after that. So I gave it a kick back toward the house with my foot.

But when I looked up, Dad was already heading inside.

"Come on, Adonis, the game is gonna start up again."

The second half was as good as the first. The score was tied at 17, with just three minutes to go.

Then Mom came into the living room and said, "Adonis, it's almost four o'clock. I need you to pick up your sister and her friends from the movies."

"No way, I'll miss the end of the game."

"Would you rather cook dinner and I'll go get them?" Mom asked in a pointed tone. "Remember, our deal about you using my car on the weekends had to do with you taking more responsibility. If you want to back out of it over a football game, that's fine."

I could see myself taking Melody out on a city bus— or worse, her driving me.

"Dad, can I at least take the Trans Am?"

"No."

"Why not? You got Mom's Honda here, in case you get a fire call."

"It's not all about that," said Dad. "The car's a fourth-generation Firebird Trans Am. Pontiac stopped making them seven years ago and is now out of business. I grew up on those cars. They're all I ever drove. I don't want to waste some of the miles it's got left so you can make a movie run. Besides, new drivers are hard on cars—the engine, brakes, dings, dents."

"I understand. You want to deny your only son the same opportunity you had growing up, to sit behind the wheel of an American classic," I said, laying on the guilt thick. "I'll probably have to settle for driving some Japanese crap one day, with a name I can't even pronounce. How do they say it—'Hi-un-dai'?"

"Here," Dad finally conceded, tossing me the keys. "And it's only because you're missing the end of the game."

"The movie's over at four oh five. They're at the Orpheum," Mom said. "They'll be waiting outside."

I didn't want to let on, but I'd trade the ending of that game for driving Dad's car anytime, especially when I could catch the highlights later on ESPN.

Dad's Firebird was white, with a single blue stripe running down the center. That was exactly the same as the Central High team colors. The car practically hugged the ground, and it had a rear spoiler and pop-up headlights. It was powerful, too, a real muscle car with a V-8 engine beneath the hood.

It had been nearly three months since I was behind

the wheel of that gorgeous baby, and that was with Dad riding shotgun. Now I was flying solo.

At a red light two blocks from the Orpheum, a pair of good-looking girls gave me the eye as they crossed the street, right in front of me. I revved the engine high and felt all that horsepower. Then, when the light turned green, I punched the gas and took off down the street like I owned it.

It was already 4:08. There were plenty of people outside the theater to see me in that sleek sports car, but Jeannie and her girlfriends were nowhere in sight.

After a few more minutes, I looked up at the marquee. There was a horror movie and two shoot-'em-up flicks playing. None of them was the kind Jeannie would go to see.

So I figured Mom had screwed up, and that they had gone to the Premiere, six or seven blocks in the opposite direction.

By the time I got there, Jeannie and her friends had walked all the way up to the corner and were starting home on their own. That's when I saw that she was with Alan and another girl.

I thought about hitting the horn to get their attention.

But I didn't want anyone seeing me drive Alan around.

What if he tried to sit up front? What if we ran into somebody from the team?

It was a no-brainer. Mom had given me the wrong theater. That was the perfect excuse. So I just let the three of them keep right on walking. And I took the long way home, looking for more girls to impress.

6

On Monday morning, I got to English class expecting Mr. D'Antoni to have us in groups, working on our projects. I was even going to have a little fun with Alan, saying something like, "I went to pick you guys up at the movies yesterday, but my mom told me the wrong theater. Hey, can I say that, you *guys?* You were right, it's funny how that works—you *guys,* you *girls.*"

Only none of that happened.

D'Antoni had the chairs arranged in regular rows, and Alan wasn't there when I walked in. Instead, D'Antoni handed out that goofy poem by Walt Whitman, the one Alan had read in our group a few days ago. The poem I'd turned over to the blank side of the page and plugged out on halfway through.

"What about the sports project?" somebody asked D'Antoni.

"That's ongoing, something we'll pick up and put down for a while. Today, I want to reread and discuss this poem together," he answered. "A week from today, you'll be responsible for handing in a one-page reaction paper on it and comparing it to another of Whitman's poems that you choose."

The assignment was barely out of D'Antoni's mouth, along with the groans of a half dozen kids, including me, when Alan arrived and took his seat.

He sat in the first row, on the far right-hand side of the room by the door, three chairs back from the front.

"See me after class about today's lateness," D'Antoni told him, walking over to put a poem down on his desk.

Within seconds, there was a buzz in the class that kept on building.

It moved like a wave from Alan's side of the room over to mine. That's when Toby got my attention, and Marshall's, too, with a sharp *pssst*. He was sitting closer to Alan than we were. Toby mouthed the word *fag* and then circled his lips with a finger.

I leaned back from the tail end of the fifth row, over by the windows, trying to get a good angle on Alan.

Then, suddenly, Alan shifted his head, and I could see it.

Alan was wearing lipstick—red, red lipstick that stood out like a stop sign against his pale skin and blond hair.

Kids in class were out-and-out snickering now, mostly the guys.

For maybe a minute, I couldn't take my eyes off Alan, even though it gave me the creeps to look at him.

"All right, everybody, settle down. I've been teaching with this ponytail for fifteen years, and no class has ever had this kind of reaction to it before," said D'Antoni, shifting the focus to himself. "You're all big boys and girls. It's just a personal decision. Accept it and move on."

All I could think in my head was, *Leave it to a hippie with a ponytail to stick up for a homo wearing lipstick.*

"Maxine, read us the first three lines of this poem," D'Antoni said. "Toby, read us the next set of three, and Adonis, the final three lines."

I hated reading out loud. I always tried to do it flat with no emotion at all, so teachers wouldn't pick me again. But at least that sickening feeling of waiting for my turn to read partly took my mind off Alan's lips.

"'Are you the new person drawn toward me? To begin with take warning, I am surely far different from what you suppose; Do you suppose you will find in me your ideal?'" said Maxine, whose bracelets made the same noise banging into each other when she sat down as they did when she'd stood up to read.

Toby didn't bother to stand up. He stayed in his seat and read, "'Do you think it so easy to have me become your lover?'"

Somebody made a kissing sound with their lips— *mwah-mwah*. And lots of kids laughed, till D'Antoni cleared his throat in an annoyed tone.

"'Do you think the friendship of me would be un-a-lloy'd satisfaction?'" Toby continued, struggling over that weird word.

That's when I went over the last three lines quick in my head to see if there was anything that would trip me up.

"'Do you think I am trusty and faithful?'" he ended.

I took a deep breath and read fast from my seat, "'Do you see no further than this façade—this smooth and tolerant manner of me? Do you suppose yourself advancing on real ground toward a real heroic man? Have you no thought O dreamer that it may be all ma-ya, illusion?'"

Just before I finished, I'd felt like kids all over the room were either tuned into my reading or staring at Alan's lips. And that wasn't the kind of company I wanted to keep.

"Good reading, all three of you. Now let's go over some of the more difficult words before we analyze this piece," said D'Antoni as I wiped a single bead of sweat from my temple.

LATER, IN THE CAFETERIA, I SAW JEANNIE ON THE LUNCH LINE, and I pushed my way through to reach her.

"So, have you seen him in that freakin' lipstick?" I asked.

"Yes, I have. Alan was wearing it yesterday at the movies. What about it?"

"And you expected me to let him in the car like that?"

"Well, then aren't you lucky you got the *wrong* information," she said in a super-sarcastic voice. "I thought Mom was picking us up. This doesn't have anything to do with you, Adonis. Alan's my friend, not yours. What do you care?"

"Because people see you hanging around with him, and that reflects on me."

"Seems you don't mind the way Melody thinks it reflects on you," she said, grabbing a plastic tray and balancing a small container of milk in one corner of it. "Why don't you tell her what you *really* think of Alan?"

I turned around to see if Melody was anywhere in earshot. Luckily, she wasn't. And when I looked back at Jeannie, she had already moved ahead without me.

"I act differently with different people. There's nothing wrong with that," I told her across that empty space between us.

"So then who are you, really—the shallow loser or

the liar? God knows who you are when it's just you and your football buddies," she said over her shoulder, without turning around to look at me.

I stood there steaming over that, as I caught my reflection in the curved aluminum crossbeams of the lunch counter. My entire body was squeezed down, short and squat, like I was looking into one of those funhouse mirrors. Only there was nothing funny about any of it.

Then the guy behind me who was waiting to move forward asked, "Are you going to get a lunch?"

But I just walked off the line without any food, and without answering him or Jeannie.

GYM WAS MY LAST PERIOD OF THE DAY, AND THAT'S WHERE I saw Alan next.

Before class, I popped open my locker and got smacked hard with the stink of old sweat. I'd forgotten to take home the gym shirt I wore Friday to be washed. And even the clean one I had in there had absorbed some of the smell.

I changed in the section reserved for varsity athletes. So Alan was a good seven or eight rows of tall lockers away, hidden from my view. But I knew when he'd got there by the comments I heard.

"Yo, the girls' locker room is across the hall."

"How was that cherry Kool-Aid—good? You need to wipe your mouth."

"Miss, your makeup's all smudged."

"I didn't know this was a coed gym class."

I was surprised when Alan didn't run his mouth back with any real gas.

He sounded almost tired when he said, "Maybe one day you'll all grow up."

And I knew when Alan had finished changing into his gym clothes, too, because the catcalls of "faggot" and "homo" followed him out the door.

Weather-wise, it was a perfect day, and class was held outside on the athletic field. We started with some easy stretching. Then the gym teacher told us to pair up and do two sets of thirty sit-ups apiece, with our partners anchoring our feet.

I grabbed another guy from the football team, and

then I watched as Alan never made a move toward anyone. Dudes moved away from him fast, like whatever he had was contagious. In the end, there was just Alan and one pencil-thin freshman without a partner.

"Let's go! Let's go! You two are together!" the gym teacher shouted at them.

"They're *together*," somebody echoed.

That freshman barely put his hands on the toes of Alan's sneakers, and Alan's feet were moving all over the place, making it twice as hard for him to do those sit-ups.

When it was the freshman's turn, Alan started out sitting right in front of him. And even though his face wasn't any closer to the kid's crotch than anybody's partner, somebody called out, "Crotch watcher. Harpring's a crotch watcher."

Some guys from the team snorted over that, including my partner.

Then the freshman closed his knees together tight, as his cheeks turned nearly as red as Alan's lips.

Kids started making kissing sounds every time that freshman did a sit-up and his face met Alan's. But after a couple of sit-ups, Alan moved off to his right side.

We were doing a volleyball unit, and the teacher had us all serving over an outdoor net. Maybe a quarter of the guys in class served underhand, like a girl. That's what I expected Alan to do when it was his turn. But he hit the ball overhand, instead, straight into the net.

"Not enough strength—you need more height on the ball. Try it like this," said the teacher, popping over an underhand serve.

"No, thank you," said Alan, who on his fourth try finally made one overhand, to a mock cheer.

After class, I stayed on the athletic field and walked some laps around the track, just not to hear that freak show surrounding Alan in the locker room.

Practice was in another twenty minutes. So I was going to have to change again anyway. But this time it was going to be surrounded by 100 percent real guys— varsity football players who thought and felt the way I did.

When I got back to the lockers, most of the guys were already there, putting on their practice jerseys.

Ethan had his shoulder pads on and was twisting off the cap to a jar of Lamp Black. Then I watched him dip a finger into it, before he painted a thick black line beneath each eye to block out the sun.

"Hey, Cap," Godfrey said to him. "Let me have some of that. I don't want to lose any of your passes in the glare."

"Yeah, me, too—it's bright out there today," followed Bishop.

"Not as bright as queer boy's lips," cracked Marshall, looking at me. "Right, Adonis? We were in English this morning when he was *fashionably late,* wearing that shit."

Toby said, "Adonis is in the same project group. You're gonna have to stare him/her/whatever in the face all period."

"Thanks for reminding me," I said, opening my locker.

"You should have to look at him as punishment," Ethan told me, with a half smile. "You're probably the one who made him feel pretty, with that compliment about his perfume."

I pulled my shoulder pads over my head, faking a laugh.

"Anyway, I had it right when I christened that boy *Alana*," said Marshall.

"Don't go taking credit," said Godfrey. "I called him that way before you did."

"How 'bout this?" Ethan interrupted. "As captain of this team, I say that we only call that homo 'Alana.' Nobody uses his right name from now on. And if you're stuck in front of a teacher or somebody else like that, just don't say anything. Agreed?"

Then Ethan put his hand out flat, facedown, in the middle of us.

We all piled our hands on top of his, and at the count of three, we called out, "Agreed!"

I WAS STARVING BY THE TIME I GOT HOME. AND WITH DAD ON duty, there was no family dinner. So Mom and Jeannie had already eaten.

Mom had made a meat loaf, with mixed vegetables on the side.

She sat across from me while I ate in the dining room, with Jeannie doing her homework at the head of the table.

"Jeannie tells me there was a little *distraction* in your English class today."

"Yeah, Al—" I said, pulling back on his name. "He's out of control. I don't know why he wants that kind of attention. Oh, and by the way, sis, I'd say he's *officially* gay now."

"I didn't know you were keeper of gay roll books," Jeannie said, before sticking a sour tongue out at me.

"It's probably not attention Alan's looking for," Mom said. "Maybe he's acting on what feels natural to him."

"Then the abuse he took today must have been pretty natural, too," I said. "He got hounded in gym class."

"You've got some Goth kids in school. I've seen them. The boys even wear dark eye makeup sometimes. Nobody reacts to it like that. Do they?" Mom asked.

"But that's pretend. They don't want to be girls. They're probably looking to score with Goth chicks," I said.

"I'm not surprised that's what you think, Adonis," Jeannie said, smug.

"I'll bet it's not as big a deal tomorrow," said Mom. "People usually accept what they get used to seeing."

"We've got a Fashion Club meeting tomorrow afternoon and another one on Wednesday," said Jeannie. "I know Alan's friends are going to support him. Lots of us have already talked it over. I just hope he doesn't have any problems with his father over this. Problems that are too big to handle."

"Oh, yeah, the colonel," I snickered. "He'll be thrilled."

"Did Alan take the lipstick off before he went home?" Mom asked.

"I know he did," answered Jeannie.

"If anybody cares, I need a Walt Whitman poem to write about."

"Try 'O Captain! My Captain!'" Jeannie said. "I read it last year in Mr. D'Antoni's class. It's very moving, with a lot to say about loss."

"'O Captain! My Captain!'" I repeated, grabbing a pen from Jeannie and writing the title down so I wouldn't forget. "We've got a team captain. That sounds like a poem I can handle."

"Don't get your hopes up, genius. It's not about football," Jeannie came back. "Although you guys do know a thing or two about losing."

Then Mom told me it was about the assassination of Abraham Lincoln.

7

When I got to English the next morning, Melody and Maxine were standing outside the classroom door.

"Adonis, I'm glad you're here," said Melody, putting her hand onto my shoulder. "Have you seen Alan yet today?"

"No, why?"

"We want to make sure he's all right," she answered. "Girls from the Fashion Club are going to try and meet him at every class and walk with him through the halls. So he doesn't get made fun of."

"Especially by some of our bonehead jocks," added Maxine.

It was funny, but the way she'd said it in front of me, I didn't believe Maxine meant me at all.

"I was thinking you could be kind of a bridge for

Alan," said Melody, sliding her hand down around to my upper arm. "Maybe you could tell some of the guys on the football team to ease up and get them to back off a little. I know they respect you."

That's when I saw Toby and Marshall, who were inside the classroom, starting over towards the door.

"Sure," I said, before my teammates got close enough to hear. "I'll help out."

"There he is," said Maxine, pointing to Alan coming down the hall with another girl.

"Thanks, you're the best. I knew you'd be cool with this," said Melody, planting a kiss on two of her fingers and then touching them to my cheek. "I've gotta run before I'm late myself."

Maxine waited for Alan. But I stepped inside quick, intercepting Toby and Marshall.

"Your girl following you to class now?" Marshall asked.

"She can't get enough of me," I told them. "I'm addictive."

"You're like her man-fix, huh?" said Marshall, running his right hand through his buzz cut.

"Well, better to see a babe like Melody here than that freak Alana," said Toby.

That's when D'Antoni began clapping his hands and announced, "Everyone, into your groups—sports projects today! You'll need to make some decisions on team names and other things!"

Once we got into our group, I couldn't look Alan in the face for more than a second or two. He was in the seat directly across from mine.

It felt like those red, red lips of his were pulsing out at me. And if they had suddenly become a hundred times bigger, reaching out across his desk on their own to plant one on me, like in some kind of crazy Bugs Bunny cartoon, I would have believed it. Only I would have pulled a gigantic rubber mallet out of my pocket and clocked him with it—*wham!* Then little yellow birdies would have been tweeting around his head to show how dizzy he was.

So I mostly kept my eyes going back and forth from Wendy's face to Maxine's whenever they talked, and staring down at Alan's hands and my own in between.

"I was thinking that Adonis is right," Alan said. "Football does get people going. Just look at all the excitement about the game here on Friday night—the posters, the morning announcements to buy tickets, the cheerleaders and marching-band practicing."

"And they don't even win much," said Maxine with a smirk.

"It's a brand-new season," I responded. "Things can change, just look around you."

I snuck a quick peek at Alan. I didn't know if he'd take that as any kind of insult. But he had a smile on his face.

"And I think we should call our team the Blaze, considering Adonis's father is a firefighter," Alan added. "Out of respect for the job he does protecting people."

"I can go for that," said Wendy. "Maybe we can have one of those fire-truck dogs, a Dalmatian, as a mascot."

"And the players can dress in bright red uniforms, with flames on their helmets," said Maxine.

I was thinking, *First he hangs out with my sister, and now he's trying to flatter my dad.* I didn't need any more of a connection to Alan than I already had. But I had to admit, all of a sudden, there was a little more of a spark in me about the project.

Then Wendy killed it when she said, "Yes, a red like the color of Alan's lipstick. I really like that shade. It's perfect for you, Alan, the way it compliments your skin tone."

"Thank you, sweetie. But truthfully, I don't have much choice. It's the only color I own."

"We'll take care of that at the Fashion Club meeting today," said Maxine, beginning to search through her oversized purple purse. "I'm sure girls will donate extra lipsticks they have. I probably have one here you can keep."

"I don't know where I'd be without my friends," said Alan as I avoided any eye contact with him.

In my mind, I had this sick image of Alan and Melody swapping lipsticks, and him wearing one she'd had on when I had kissed her.

I watched the manicured fingernails of Alan's right hand as he picked up a blue pen. At the top of a clean sheet of paper he wrote our four names. Then he wrote, *The Blaze will be a professional football team playing in the city of Cincinnati, Ohio, which had the first full-time fire department.*

"Adonis, who's doing the writing for your group again?" D'Antoni asked from his desk.

"Right there," I answered, pointing at Alan, who'd already raised his free hand.

I caught Marshall's and Toby's eye and nodded to them, just to show I hadn't used Alan's name, or even a *he* or *him*.

BEFORE GYM CLASS THAT AFTERNOON, THERE WEREN'T ANY comments about Alan in the locker room. An extra gym teacher, with his arms folded across his chest and a whistle hanging down around his neck, stood watch over the row of lockers where Alan was changing. Only it was just the two of them, because every other guy who'd had a locker in that row moved somewhere else.

It was the same after class, too.

It was like Alan had his own special section now.

But it wasn't marked off by a sign that read VARSITY ATHLETES.

And I was thinking if there was a sign for him it would have read PRIME-TIME FREAK.

TUESDAY WAS THE LAST REAL FOOTBALL PRACTICE, WITH PADS and hitting, before the game on Friday night. Wednesday would just be a walk-through of everything we'd learned. Then on Thursday, we'd have the day off, as our coach said, "To let it all sink into our bodies and brains."

Near the end of practice, at about four thirty, I saw Dad sitting in the bleachers alone.

He'd seen most of my games last year, trading shifts with guys at work when he had to. I'd never felt nervous playing in front of him before. But there was something about him being the only one up there that had me pressing on the field.

It was just his eyes on me.

We finished practice with a fumble drill, in groups of three.

It was me, Marshall, and Toby standing ready in a

semicircle, as our offensive-line coach tossed the ball onto the ground.

The three of us pounced, scrapping and clawing to get ahold of it.

Then, suddenly, I found myself at the bottom of the pile with the ball tucked away beneath me, against my belly.

When the whistle blew, I stood up with it, raising that pigskin high, like a trophy, for Dad to see. He was already clapping. And I spiked that ball to the ground, doing a little bit of my celebration dance.

After practice, I grabbed my bag fast and raced over to the bleachers to go home with Dad, still wearing my jersey and pads.

He tossed me the keys to his car and said, "Here, you drive."

As I was warming up the engine to the Firebird, he said, "You know I played a little junior varsity baseball in high school. But the only time my father ever saw me play was when I was hitting a stickball with a broom handle in the street outside our apartment building.

And that was probably because he'd stuck his head out the window to scream at me that my mother needed her broom back."

"That's terrible, Dad. Doesn't sound like you two were very close."

"Yeah, and he died before I ever made anything of myself—my job, my family," Dad said. "I just want you to know I'm proud of you. Playing varsity football is really something, the way you fight out there like a man. You're doing all the right things in my book."

"Thanks."

"Maybe you *should* consider joining the military. I think you can handle it. You might be the kind of man they're looking for."

"Hey, maybe I am."

I drove us home feeling like an all-American and not just a starter on the offensive line of a losing high-school football team.

Pulling up to our house, I saw Melody's car in the driveway again.

Then Dad pointed to it and said, "That's another reason I'm proud of you, son. I've seen her around with your sister. That's some good-looking girl you've got."

I stepped out of the Firebird like I was walking on air, and I even had to turn myself sideways a little to fit through our front door in my shoulder pads.

Mom called out from the kitchen as me and Dad walked inside, "Boys, we have company upstairs. Adonis, I need to tell you—"

"He already knows, dear," Dad cut her off, winking at me as I started up the stairs.

I could hear high-pitched voices laughing and carrying on as I headed up to my room. Jeannie's bedroom door was open. I knew it would be. That was Mom's number-one rule about having friends over: the door to your room could never be shut when you were inside with them.

I stopped a few feet away and listened.

"He's really cute. I've always had a crush on him."

"How about his brother?"

"I know. They're total opposites. Can you believe they came from the same parents?"

Barclay was inside Jeannie's room, too. He must have picked up my scent, because I heard his collar jingling as he ran towards me. So I stepped beneath the archway, knocking on Jeannie's open door.

My sister, Melody, and Maxine were all sitting on the bed.

That's when Jeannie, in a deep voice, like a narrator from the History Channel, said, "It's the manly warrior returning from the battlefield of football practice."

Melody and Maxine cracked up over that, and I laughed along, too.

"He could be in a commercial holding a stick of deodorant right now," joked Maxine.

Melody, who'd stood up and started over to me, added, "And the tagline would be 'Cover up the Central High Wildcat in you.'"

When she got up close, Melody whispered, "I'm sorry, Adonis. I know it's not cool for you to come home and just find me at your house. But we—"

"No, it's fine," I said, breaking in. "Fashion Club stuff, I understand. You don't have to worry about it. I'm gonna go hit the shower now before I really stink up the place."

"I'm only going to be here a few more minutes anyway. I've got to drive other people home," she said, sending me off with a soft push.

I grabbed a robe from my room, ditching my football cleats and socks.

Then I took a fresh towel from the linen closet and headed down the hall towards the bathroom. Every step I took was sure and confident. I was convinced things couldn't get any better for me. I was fantasizing about what it would be like to shower with Melody, to soap up every one of her curves. But just as I reached for the bathroom doorknob, it turned open from the other side.

Alan walked out.

For a second, I was frozen solid, looking down at his bright red lips. I must have surprised him, too, because he stared eye level into the uniform number on my jersey, taking a half step back, like he was ready to run from it.

"Oh, Adonis, it's you," he said with his hand over his heart.

"Everything all right?" Jeannie yelled from her room.

"Yes! Yes! Your brother needs the bathroom. That's all," he said, stepping around me. "I'm finished."

I stood there staring straight ahead at the blue sea-shell shower curtain.

Then I looked back down the hall to see Alan down on one knee and Barclay on his back. Alan was scratching Barclay's belly, and that dog's hind legs were spinning through the air faster than I'd ever seen. And everything Ethan had said about Barclay turning homo went roaring through my brain.

I walked into the bathroom without saying a word, and I closed the door behind me. I thought that would end it. But it didn't. I'd just put myself into a space where Alan been alone for at least five minutes, doing God knows what.

I checked out the sink and peered into the trash,

ready to recoil from anything with a lipstick smudge on it.

Then I lifted the toilet seat with my foot, before I sprayed it with Lysol.

I turned the hot water on in the shower, thinking that would sanitize things. But as the bathroom filled up with steam, and mirror fogged over, it felt like the room was shrinking and everything was closing in on me.

I started to undress. Then I stopped to check the lock on the door, just to make sure. Finally, I jumped into the shower. And by the time I heard them all going downstairs, and then Melody's car start up in the driveway, I was lathered up with soap from head to toe.

Maybe twenty minutes later, wearing a T-shirt and sweatpants, I headed downstairs ready to blast Jeannie for not warning me about *him*.

"Hey, sis! What's wrong with you?"

I heard the *clink* of dinner plates in the dining room, and I marched past Dad, who was sitting alone on the living room couch watching TV.

Then I turned the corner and saw Alan, still wearing his lipstick, helping Jeannie set the table.

It hit me right away: there were five settings instead of four.

"I don't know, Adonis, *what's* wrong with me?" she said.

Mom came in from the kitchen holding a tray of spaghetti and meatballs, and said in her stern voice, "Whatever's between you two, put it away. We have company."

"It's all right," said Alan, glaring straight at me. "I love the communication your family has. I understand exactly what *everybody's* thinking."

"We do have plenty of that around here, Alan," Mom said, who also had a pointed look for me. "But when I spoke to your father on the phone about you staying for dinner, he seemed like someone who could communicate very well."

"More like interrogate," he said, folding one of our red cloth napkins in a fancy way, then standing it up on the table. "There, a rose—everything but the smell."

"It's so beautiful," said Jeannie. "How did you learn to do that?"

"My grandmother taught me," Alan said. "Tomorrow would have been her eighty-fifth birthday."

I slid down into my seat knowing I wasn't going to have much of an appetite.

Then Dad walked in, stone silent, and took his place at the head of the table. Mom sat opposite Dad, and Jeannie was across from me, with Alan sitting next to her.

"Alan, what was your grandmother like?" asked Mom.

"Oh, she was an incredible woman. I owe her so much. She taught me how to take care of myself—to cook and sew, and in other ways, too. My grandmother even worked as a welder once in a shipyard during the Second World War. Can you imagine?"

"Alan was raised by her, while his father was away in the military," Jeannie said, almost directly to Dad, like she was catching him up on a movie he'd come in on halfway through.

"How about that," said Dad, trying to look interested.

"Adonis, did you tell your father we named our project team the Blaze, in honor of him being a firefighter?" Alan asked.

"No, not yet," I answered, watching Alan suck in three long strands of spaghetti and dab the tomato sauce from his red lips with a napkin. "But I guess he knows now."

"A nice tribute," Mom said for Dad, who feigned a smile.

After a minute of silence, Dad asked, "So Alan, what about your mother?"

"Alan didn't offer us that, dear," Mom chided. "He hasn't mentioned her."

"It's all right," Alan said, before taking a deep breath. "She abandoned me when I was very young. She had drug and alcohol problems. I don't know where she is."

"I'm sorry," said Jeannie, dropping her hand on top of his.

"I almost never talk about her, not even at home. To my father, she doesn't exist anymore," said Alan. "I guess there's something about sitting around a dinner table with a real family that puts me at ease. I feel like I could talk about anything here."

"Okay, why are you wearing that lipstick?" Dad asked, flat-out.

Jeannie and Mom were both yelling at Dad when Alan answered, "It's who I am."

"And who's that?" I asked, before I'd even realized the words had left my mouth.

"I'm not completely sure," Alan said. "But I know I'm getting closer to finding out. The lipstick's just a part of it."

Right then, I would have given anything to be part of some student-exchange program. Alan could have come to dinner at our house, and I would have been eating with the colonel. I know Dad would have come along with me if he had the chance. We probably could have heard a bunch of war stories about tanks and big guns, instead of the sickening crap that was ringing in my ears now.

When dinner was over and the table got cleared by the *girls*, Mom said she was going to drive Alan home. I'd already made sure to mention how much homework

I had, so I wouldn't get trapped into driving him.

Before he left, Alan went upstairs to the bathroom.

"He's has to take the lipstick off," Jeannie said. "He can't go home with it on. I think that's really sad."

That's when Dad and me threw each other a look, like if we had our way, we both would have hosed Alan clean in the front yard before he ever stepped into the house.

8

The next day, when I got to D'Antoni's class, Maxine and Alan were talking just inside the door. They were each wearing long green scarves, and I wanted to kick myself for actually noticing that Alan's was a shade darker.

I ducked my head and slipped past them both to see Toby and Marshall standing over by Marshall's desk.

I'd cocked my arm in the air to give those guys high fives when Alan called out to me, "Adonis, I want to thank you and your family for dinner last night, and for having such an open ear. You and I are making progress, you know."

As Alan's words sank in, it felt like the floor had been yanked out from beneath me. Suddenly, I didn't know how or where to take my next step. My arm shrank back down and I laid my palm flat on Marshall's desk for support.

"All right," I said, without ever turning my head around towards him. "It's my sister's fault," I whispered to Toby and Marshall.

"Which one?" Toby replied low. "Jeannie or *Alana?*"

Before I could explain it, D'Antoni arrived and hustled us all into our seats.

Then, just a minute or two into the lesson, Marshall turned to me and mouthed the word *dinner?*

I could almost see the bad taste in his mouth and the huge question mark formed behind it with his lips.

Marshall didn't look over my way again.

For the next forty minutes I felt that weight. It was like I was struggling to get some heavy bar off my chest while I was pumping iron, without a teammate to spot for me.

When the bell finally rang, I packed up my books and started towards Marshall's desk. But Alan was on his way over to me waving a piece of paper.

"Here, I know your father would appreciate a copy

of our project plan. It has all our names on it. And I put yours up at the top," he said through his painted lips. "I feel like I owe it to him for having me in his house."

I wanted to stamp my finger down on his name and scream out at the top of my lungs, *You've got it wrong. You screwed up your own name. It's Alana Harpring. Alana! You hear me? Alana!*

Then there wouldn't have been a question mark in anybody's mind where I stood.

That ponytailed D'Antoni would have sent me to the dean's office. And when my parents got the call, there would have been hell to pay at home with Mom, and Jeannie, too. I knew Dad would have gone much easier on me.

But I didn't scream any of that stuff.

I told myself it was mainly because of Melody, and how she would have seen me for some big phony.

But it really wasn't.

It was because I knew it would crush Alan, maybe not on the outside, where I'd be able to see it, but on the inside, where it counts.

Only I didn't want to admit that to myself then.

"Uh, thanks. You really didn't have to do that," I said, snatching the paper from his hand, with Marshall and Toby watching us from the door, before they split without me.

A FEW PERIODS LATER, I GOT TO THE CAFETERIA AS EARLY AS I could, and I grabbed a seat around the team's usual table. I must have been sitting there for five or six minutes by myself while the cafeteria filled up with students. And I even started to second-guess that I had the right table and lunch period, like I was lost in an episode of *The Twilight Zone*.

Then, the guys almost all showed up at once, with Ethan leading the pack.

Bishop and Godfrey took seats on either side of me. Toby and Marshall sat across the way.

Only Ethan stayed on his feet, looking down at me.

"As team captain, I don't normally address rumors," he said in a serious tone. "But it's come to my attention that *Alana* Harpring may have thanked you in front of an entire class for having an 'open rear.'"

"What?" I hollered, rising up.

"It could have been an 'open *ear*,'" said Marshall, beginning to smile.

"I was there," said Toby, trying to keep a straight face. "I'm not sure which it was."

"See what you leave yourself wide open for," said Ethan, dropping a hand on my shoulder as I lowered myself back down. "Just from hanging around that queer."

"But I did hear 'dinner,'" said Marshall. "That's for sure."

"Was there candlelight, too?" Bishop asked me.

"Nah, not on a first date," cracked Godfrey.

"How do we know it was their *first* date?" Toby piled on.

"Look, my whole family was there. My mom served spaghetti and meatballs," I said.

"Meat *what*?" asked Bishop.

But I knew what was coming about *balls*, and I wouldn't bite at his stupid joke.

"It's my sister's fault. She's in the Fashion Club with that misfit," I tried to explain. "Then all of a sudden Melody's involved."

"That's why you've got to wear the pants in a relationship from the start," Ethan said to me. "You should've took care of that last Saturday night, when you *nailed* that picture up in her house. You showed her that *hammer*, right?"

I nodded my head, lying to myself as much as anybody else.

"So she knows," Ethan kept on. "She's not gonna trade you for some fag friend. And what was Jeannie going to do if you skipped dinner? Nothing—she's your blood."

Then Ethan headed for the lunch line, and everybody else but me followed. I stayed glued to my seat, worried that if I got up I'd lose my place at the table, maybe forever.

When everybody got back with their trays of food, Bishop asked, "Adonis, aren't you going to eat?"

"No, I've got a lot on my mind," I answered.

"If it's not Wildcat football, get rid of it," Ethan said.

"We don't need you thinking too much at the game on Friday night. You just nail those dudes on the line from Park Heights flat."

"If you're not eating, maybe you should find Melissa Henry," Toby said.

"The head cheerleader? Why?" I asked.

"Sign her petition. She got all freaked out about having to sit next to lipstick boy in social studies," Godfrey said. "So this morning she started one to get him either kicked out of school or put in his own class. Something like fifty kids signed it already."

"It's got my John Hancock," said Marshall.

"Mine, too," added Bishop. "In big bold letters."

Then Ethan told me, "Putting your name on that petition would set things straight. No more confusion in anybody's head where you stand on the issue."

"I guess you're right. Time to put my signature where my mouth is," I said before I left the table.

But I walked across the crowded cafeteria knowing I could never sign that petition. Not unless I scribbled my name so bad that nobody would be able to read it.

So instead of finding Melissa Henry, I hung a quick

left into the boys' bathroom. I closed a stall door behind me and just sat on the toilet, thinking, and dealing with the stink of other people's shit and piss.

There was some graffiti written on the back of the stall door in black Magic Maker.

IN GRAMMAR SCHOOL THEY TAUGHT YOU TO WASH YOUR HANDS AFTER TAKING A SHIT. BY NOW YOU SHOULD HAVE LEARNED TO STOP SHITTING ON YOUR HANDS, ASSHOLE.

And I kept reading it to myself, over and over, waiting for the changing bell.

DURING WARM-UP IN GYM CLASS, THE TEACHER PUT OUT maybe a dozen jump ropes. So I picked one up and tried to work on my form. I made seven jumps on my first go at it, and eight the second time. And I felt less like an ape, with my feet starting to get lighter beneath me.

I was catching my breath, getting ready to go again, when Alan grabbed a rope off the ground.

"That was pretty good, Adonis," he said. "But you

need more speed in your hands. If you turn the rope faster, you'll jump much smoother and find a rhythm."

"Is that right?" I said with some attitude.

"Like this," he said, setting his red sneakers together and clicking his heels, like Dorothy from *The Wizard of Oz*. "Don't worry. I think *the guys* will accept you taking jump-rope lessons from me."

But Alan didn't jump rope like a little girl. He jumped more like a boxer, first off the right foot for a while, and then the left. And the rope kept spinning faster, until it sounded like a whirlwind growing inside my ears. By the time he'd quit, my shoulders had shrunk down to nothing.

"Wow," I said, dropping my rope and walking off.

From that moment on, I knew I was finished with all that nonsense about learning to jump rope. I wasn't about to be behind Alan at anything athletic.

Football practice that afternoon was just a walk-through. Nobody wore pads or helmets, and we concentrated on getting every formation right.

I got down into my stance on the offensive line, with the knuckles from one hand on the ground for balance. Marshall and Toby were on the line with me. Godfrey and Bishop were spread out wide as receivers. And Ethan was standing over the center, barking out signals.

In my head, I knew all of my blocking assignments and responsibilities.

I was just waiting for Ethan to say, "Hut-hut," for the center to snap him the ball.

But before he did, Ethan moved from under center and put his hands beneath my backside instead. It was the last thing I ever expected, and I jumped offsides, over the line of scrimmage, with the rest of my teammates howling.

"Did you think I was your favorite dinner date?" Ethan said, and then paused. "Melody."

I knew he could have said "Alana" and got an even bigger laugh.

"I told you, you need to get these *females* off your mind," he said. "Now let's get back to football. There's a game to win, and you're a big part of my protection."

We all got set again. Then when Ethan called the

signal, I exploded off the line through an imaginary defender. I was hyped, like I had something to prove now. I did that for the rest of our plays, with some real aggression.

Before we went inside to change, Coach reminded us about relaxing on our day off tomorrow, letting everything we'd just practiced become a part of us.

There was a Fashion Club meeting that afternoon. So I didn't look for a ride home from Ethan or anybody else, in case Jeannie had another surprise waiting for me.

I took my time walking, too, going over all the different things I could do or say if Alan was really there again. But when I got home, only Mom's car was in the driveway.

From the living room, I could hear voices upstairs. And after I'd called out, "Mom? Jeannie?" a door slammed shut.

When I got up there, Barclay was sitting in front of Jeannie's closed bedroom door. I heard Jeannie's and Mom's muffled voices inside. I was positive one of them said Alan's name, so I put my ear closer to the door, and Barclay let out a *woof*.

"Adonis, this is private!" Jeannie hollered, and I backed off.

Maybe ten minutes later, they both came out acting like nothing had happened.

I tried to let it go at first, but after a while I felt like I needed to know.

Later on, Mom passed by my room while I was looking up that Whitman poem about Abe Lincoln on my laptop, so I called her in.

"How's the poetry going?" she asked, looking at the screen over my shoulder.

"It's pretty depressing. Can he say 'cold and dead' one more time?"

"Yeah, it was never one of my favorites," she said, putting her fingers on the keyboard to search something new. "Try this by Whitman, 'Song of Myself.' I've always liked it. 'I celebrate myself, and sing myself. And what I assume you shall assume. For every atom belonging to me as good belongs to you.'"

"What's it about?"

"It means deep down, at the core, we're all the same. You'll probably get more out of this one."

Then I asked her what was going on with Jeannie.

"You'll have to ask your sister," she answered. "It's her story to share, not mine."

"I heard about the petition against Alan. It's not that, is it?" I asked.

"No, and that's just awful. Don't let anyone talk you into signing. I'd be more than disappointed," Mom said with some real emotion. "I swear, sometimes I think my third graders have more tolerance than teenagers in high school. Probably because they don't feel the peer pressure yet."

"Hey, I haven't even seen that petition. I've only heard other kids talking about it," I said, trying to defend myself. "And I don't bend to peer pressure. You don't see me following the crowd on anything."

Mom gave me a funny look, like she was listening to a stranger talk.

Then before she left, she said, "That's a strong, positive image to have of yourself, Adonis. Just remember, it's harder to do than say."

If Dad was home, he would have found out what was up from Mom or Jeannie for sure. Then, with a little work, I'd have pried it loose from him. But Dad was on duty at the firehouse. So it was all on me now.

After dinner, I found Jeannie alone in her room doing homework.

I walked in as nonchalant as I could.

She was sitting on her bed, surrounded by books, when I asked, "What's with all the closed-door conversation around here? Did Alan decide to change the color of his lipstick?"

"That's the reason!" Jeannie exploded, jumping up off the bed, with a few of her books falling to the floor. "It's that kind of stupidity that lets me know I can't trust you with any of this! Just go!"

I kept my mouth shut and sucked it up as I left her room.

I didn't mention Alan again. And for the rest of the night, I was walking on eggshells around her.

9

The next morning, as I approached D'Antoni's classroom, I saw Jeannie, Melody, and Maxine walking towards me from the opposite end of the hallway. It looked like there was another girl with them, one I didn't recognize at first.

Then it hit me all at once—it wasn't another girl, it was Alan wearing a dress.

I don't know what kinds of thoughts were inside my head, because they were completely scrambled. And I acted on instinct—self-preservation.

I bolted inside the classroom and headed for my seat, passing Toby without saying a single word. I opened my English notebook and stood it up in front of me to hide my face. Then I gripped the sides of my desk, like

I could feel the vibrations of an earthquake building in the ground.

I'd opened the page to our project notes, where it said *Cincinnati/Queen City*, and I'd drawn long girly eyelashes on the *ee* of *Queen*.

So I let go of the desk just long enough to flip to a different page.

Then I heard the first gasp in the room. For a second, I almost felt like it was me on trial, instead of Alan.

I raised my head up and saw Jeannie and Melody standing at the door, looking in my direction, as Alan walked inside with Maxine. But right then, I didn't want to lock eyes with either one of them and risk what they might see in me. So I lowered my head back down till I was sure they'd gone.

Even with D'Antoni clearing his throat for quiet, kids couldn't help but comment.

"Holy crap."

"It's not Halloween yet."

"Yes, it is. Trick or treat."

Alan was wearing a long black dress, with a red belt that matched his lipstick. And I followed some silvery glitter on that dress all the way down to his bare ankles, and what looked to me like black ballet slippers on his feet.

Alan was in his seat, staring straight ahead, copying the notes off the board.

Then in a calm and steady voice, to no one in particular, Alan said, "This is who I am. Get used to it. It's not going to change."

From across the room, my eyes caught Toby's.

He looked me dead square in the face, shaking his head from side to side in disgust. I nodded back to him. Then I faked shoving a finger inside my mouth, like I would gag myself and puke right there over the sight of Alan.

Marshall was the only one late for class.

But a minute later, after D'Antoni had started his lesson, Marshall came through the door. He dropped a late pass on D'Antoni's desk and walked right past Alan to his seat. I guess Marshall didn't notice him, or thought Alan was really some new girl, because it was another twenty or thirty seconds until Marshall suddenly said, "Oh, no. No, that's not right, dude."

That's when one of the school guidance counselors appeared at D'Antoni's door and said, "Excuse me for interrupting, Mr. D'Antoni, but I'd like to see, uh, Harpring for a few minutes."

He didn't call him "Alan," or "Mr. Harpring"— just "Harpring," like he was in the military or something.

"This is still *my* class time with this student," D'Antoni told the counselor, sounding like he was running interference for Alan. "Why don't you see him during lunch or study hall?"

But Alan stood up and said, "It's all right. I expected something like this. I suppose lots of people think I need *help*."

After Alan and the counselor left the classroom, D'Antoni said, "Okay, this is our opportunity to talk. Let's get all our feelings out in the open, and hopefully we can move past it. Who's got something to say?"

"It's sick," said Marshall. "Sick and perverted. I don't want to be near it."

"I'm definitely signing that petition now," said a girl in class. "This is too much."

"I can't take being in the same room with him. I wasn't raised that way," a dude said.

Then D'Antoni said, "I'll ask you all, are these our own fears talking? Do our responses have more to do with us than with Alan?"

And I hated how hippie D'Antoni had said "us" and "our," like my mind, or Toby's or Marshall's, was the same as his.

There were ten or so seconds of silence before Wendy said, "Well, I think it's brave of him. Maybe the bravest thing I've ever seen in my life."

"Brave?" mocked Toby.

"Yeah," Maxine snapped. "Braver than going out on a football field covered from head to toe in padding. We can't even see your face inside that helmet."

"That's so they can hide those lines of black makeup they put on under their eyes," said another girl.

"Definitely brave," said Maxine.

Maybe there were even some guys in the room who thought that way, too. But I could almost guarantee none of them was going to say it out loud.

"I think he likes the attention. And because of that we have to suffer," said Marshall. "He doesn't have to act like this."

"Alan doesn't have a choice," said Maxine. "This is who he is."

"Exactly," added Wendy. "He's really female. He was put in the wrong body."

"God doesn't make those kinds of mistakes," said another girl, flat-out. "That's why he's God, the Almighty."

"She's right," someone else backed her up.

"Adonis, you look like you've got something to say," D'Antoni said.

I felt like the hippie bastard just sucker punched me, putting me on the spot like that. Whatever the expression had been on my face, I changed it fast by pushing my lips together tight. Then I shook my head hard, till my neck hurt, and said, "Not me. You got the wrong guy."

D'Antoni eventually went back to his lesson, and class ended before Alan ever came back.

———

A FEW PERIODS LATER, DURING THE CHANGE, I RAN INTO MY sister in the hall.

"I guess I know what yesterday's big secret was about," I told her. "And so does everybody else in school by now."

That's when Jeannie pulled me off to the side and said, "We were having Fashion Club at Carla Daniels's house, and she was putting together this dress she'd designed. Alan's the same height as her, so he put it on to model while she worked on it."

I raised an open palm in front of my face to stop her, like I was traffic cop at an intersection, and said, "I'm not interested."

But she kept on going anyway.

"Then Alan said how comfortable he felt wearing it in front of us. Everybody applauded, and he looked so happy. Carla told him to keep the dress and gave him a pair of flats to go with it. He wore the outfit for the rest of the meeting and only took it off to go home," Jeannie finished.

"That's crazy," I said. "Why would you girls do that?"

"Nobody *did* anything. It just happened," she said.

"Well, you know what? It didn't just happen while he was surrounded by a group of guys. Did it?"

"I don't know why I even bother trying to explain things to you."

Then we both stepped back into the flow of kids through the hall, and that tide took us in different directions.

That afternoon in the cafeteria, Ethan was holding court.

"It's a nice little circus with that freak show walking around in a dress," he said. "Good entertainment on the day before the game. But I don't want to see any of this shit tomorrow. That's our time. We're going to be the main attraction, not little Miss Alana."

"I heard that since this morning, there's another two hundred names on the petition. I'll bet they kick him out and send him to one of those transvestite schools," said Godfrey.

"Yeah, which one, *Tranny High?*" mocked Bishop.

"Anywhere but here would be all right with me," said Toby, peeling a banana. "I'm just uncomfortable around that she-dude. What if he was sitting at the next table in that dress, about to deep-throat this banana? Tell me you wouldn't have to get up and move."

Then Marshall, who'd been eating lunch, pulled a plastic spork from his mouth and in a frustrated voice asked, "What's with all these females on his side, walking him to class? What that hell is that?"

"Some of them are happy to flip him over to their side," said Ethan, catching my eye. "It's a power play, pure and simple. These same girls want to manipulate all the guys in their life. They want to be in control. It's a need, strictly a female one."

"You should have seen that half-a-she-dude D'Antoni try to tug Adonis across the line this morning," said Marshall. "D'Antoni probably knows his sister and Melody are part of that fashion crew. It was 'Oh, Adonis, you look like you've got something to say.' But our boy gave him the stiff arm, and knocked his ponytailed ass backward."

"He wanted me to be the *one* guy to stick up for 'Harpring,'" I said, using my fingers to make fake quotations marks in the air when I said Alan's last name.

"Believe me, whatever little bit of respect I had for D'Antoni is gone. He ranks nowhere with me now."

"Good man, Adonis," Ethan said with his mouth half full of food. "Good man."

I walked into the boys' locker room before gym class, not knowing what I was going to find. There was no gym teacher guarding Alan's section of lockers. And there was no Alan, either. Still, he was the only thing guys were talking about.

"You didn't think they were going to let him change with us, did ya?"

"That's right, nobody would have undressed with him in here."

"No way."

"I would have done gym in my street clothes. That kind of demerit wouldn't stick."

When I got out onto the athletic field I saw Alan sitting alone in the bleachers, still wearing that black dress. I had no idea why he was up there. Maybe they were going to transfer him into a girls' gym class, or maybe they were waiting to order him a gym uniform with a skirt.

"He's probably sitting out because he's on his period," somebody said. "Pretend he's invisible, not even there."

There was a kid standing around who'd just got over the flu and had a doctor's note to be excused from gym. But once a teacher told him he had to sit in the bleachers with Alan, the kid decided to put on his uniform and participate.

All class long, I tried my best to ignore Alan and pretend he wasn't there.

The times I did sneak a peek over at him, Alan was watching us practice volleyball. He even came down off the bleachers to toss a ball back after one got away. And I just know I would have felt better if he'd been ignoring us, too.

That night, Dad was off. We ate together as a family at six thirty on the nose. Jeannie didn't get home until about ten minutes before.

"Sorry I'm late," she said, hurrying into the dining room. "I was with a few of the girls from the Fashion Club. We were making Alan a care package out of some of our old clothes and new makeup we bought him."

"Glad to see the allowance I give you is going toward *charity*," sniped Dad.

"I'm happy you approve," said Jeannie, short.

"That's the allowance *we* give her, dear," Mom called out from the kitchen.

The smell of the roast coming from there had me salivating. And I could hear Barclay's nails on the hard kitchen floor, where he was probably pacing in front of the oven door.

I'd already done Jeannie's job setting the table, and was sitting down with Dad when she switched all the forks from the right side of the plates, where I'd put them, over to the left.

"I've been talking to your brother about it," Dad said to her. "I hear it was some strange day at school."

"I think *strange* is kind of insulting to Alan," Jeannie said, sitting down.

"Really, what would you call it?" I asked her.

"Special," she answered. "It was freeing for Alan. He said so."

"Believe me, it was a sideshow. The only thing missing was the bearded lady," I told Dad. "You should have seen him sitting in the bleachers during gym in that dress. It was disturbing."

"If the school had a place for Alan to change into his gym clothes, it wouldn't have been like that," said Jeannie. "They didn't have a bathroom for him either. He was afraid to use the boys' room. So Alan had to hold it in all day. Somebody needs to start a petition over *that*."

"Dad, what if you got to a fire and somebody like Alan needed mouth-to-mouth? Would you give him the kiss of life?" I asked.

"Your father would save him, of course," Mom said, stepping into the dining room carrying the vegetables and rolls.

"It's part of the training, son," Dad answered. "You learn to react instead of think. And if all else fails, there's that plastic mouthpiece you can use, to insulate yourself from the victim."

Jeannie looked down at the blouse she was wearing and said, "Aaggh, I forgot to put this in with the rest. Alan always said how much he liked it."

"Hey, that looks almost new," said Dad with his brow curled. "You keep it."

"Remember, sweetie, Alan's not a Barbie Doll for you girls to play dress-up with," Mom said in a much softer tone. "This must be very difficult for him. Does his father know about what he wore to school today?"

"No, Alan wouldn't let the guidance counselors call him," Jeannie said. "He told them he'd probably be living out in the street if his father found out."

"Yeah, I'll bet *the colonel* takes no prisoners," I cracked.

"Not funny, Adonis," Mom said.

"You don't know how lucky we are to have parents who accept us, no matter what," Jeannie said to me. "Don't take it for granted."

"Dad, if I came home in a skirt, would it be all right with you?" I joked.

"Just make sure it's after tomorrow," he said. "I already swapped shifts with O'Reilly to be at your football game. They might not let you play if you dressed like that."

It felt great to know Dad was going to be there, and I said, "About that skirt, I'll make it a kilt. We're something like one-tenth Scottish, right?"

Then Mom asked, "So where did Alan get dressed this morning? Not at home?"

"At Maxine's," Jeannie answered.

"Well, don't volunteer our house," I said.

Jeannie just scowled at me.

"So are you girls getting your jollies out of seeing every guy at school squirm around him?" I asked her.

"We're not getting anything out of it. Alan's our friend. We want him to be himself and happy," Jeannie answered. "Who are your friends? Do they accept the real you, or do you have to put on some kind of an act all the time?"

"I don't have to sweat that," I said. "It just so happens that me and my friends think and feel exactly alike."

"You're fooling yourself, Adonis. That can't be true," said Mom, heading back into the kitchen for the pot roast.

"Melody, too?" asked Jeannie. "You think exactly the same?"

"That's totally different," I said.

"So what name does he want to go by now?" Dad asked. "Not Alan."

"Some football donkey called him 'Alana' as a put-down," answered Jeannie. "Alan said he actually liked the sound of it. But he's not sure yet."

Mom came back in with the roast, with Barclay on her heels. And she looked at me hard.

"What? There are forty-five guys on the football team," I said. "I don't control how they act."

"Or how they think and feel?" Jeannie poked at me.

That's when Jeannie's cell phone rang.

"It's Melody," she said, looking at Dad. "She drove Alan home. I just want to make sure everything's all right."

"One minute. That's all," said Dad, tucking a napkin into the collar of his shirt.

Jeannie disappeared into the living room for about thirty seconds. Then she came back and said, "Adonis, Melody wants to know if she can say something to you real quick."

Dad nodded his head to me and I took the phone.

"Hello?"

"Adonis, I'm sorry to call at dinner, but I just wanted you to know that Alan told me having you in English class this morning really meant something to him. With you there, he felt like he could at least turn his back on those other football players in the room," she said.

"Uh, that's great," I said. "Glad to hear it."

"Good luck in the game tomorrow night. I'll be watching. Bye."

"Bye, Mel," I said, before I closed the phone and handed it back to Jeannie.

10

From the moment I woke up on Friday, I was focused on the game that night. Everything else took a backseat. I hardly interacted with anybody in my family, skipping breakfast. And my time in school moved so fast, it felt like a blur.

Alan was less of a spectacle in English, at least for me. He wore another dress. This one was blue and white. But I pushed the sight of him as far out of my mind as I could, and got in and out of class quick without having to talk to anybody about it.

He participated in gym wearing a boy's uniform—shorts and a T-shirt. But that didn't stop his lips from glowing red.

Somebody said Alan had changed in the teachers' bathroom inside the gym office.

"I couldn't care less," I said, heading onto the athletic field. "It's got nothing to do with my life."

I didn't want to waste an ounce of energy on him or stupid outdoor volleyball. And I was thrilled when my team lost its class-tournament game, and I was able to kick back in the grass, facing the opposite way, while the winners kept on playing.

At the far end of the athletic field, an assistant football coach was already chalking in the lines and yard markers for our game.

While I was watching him, I tugged some grass out of the ground and tossed it up into the breeze. That's when I remembered D'Antoni once talking about a poem by his hippie king Whitman. A poem that claimed you could see the whole world in a single blade of grass. So I reached down and pulled one up to look at it close. Only there was nothing to see, because it was exactly the same from top to bottom, just like all the rest of them.

I raised that piece of grass to my mouth to make a whistle, like when I was a kid. But before I could fill my lungs, the gym teacher blew his metal whistle instead.

The volleyball game was over. The team Alan was playing on had won.

And those guys were exchanging high fives with everyone except him.

I GOT HOME FROM SCHOOL AND GRABBED MYSELF A PLATE OF cold pasta from the fridge.

Dad was already there, and Mom came in just after me.

"So who was dressed up as what today?" Dad asked. "Anybody else switch sides?"

"I ignored all that nonsense," I answered. "I've got more important business."

Then I went up to eat alone in my room, with family dinner being canceled because of the game. I was starting to shut things out around me and get my game face on. When I finished eating, I stretched out on the bed and closed my eyes for twenty minutes to rest. Then I paced around my room for a while, listening to heavy metal.

I went downstairs with the buds to my iPod in my ears.

And I hollered over the music, "I'm leaving. I'll catch you both at the game."

I saw Mom's and Dad's mouths moving from the living room, and I waved good-bye to whatever they'd said back.

Barclay was asleep by the front door. He was chasing something in a dream. His body was twitching, and all four of his legs were in high gear. And he was both whimpering and growling at the same time.

I didn't want to wake Barclay up. So I stepped over him, opened the door about a third of the way, and managed to slip out sideways.

Then I began the four-block walk to the school with the music blaring inside my head. After a while, my steps got synchronized to the rhythm of what I was listening to, and my heart was beating along to the bass.

It was nearly five o'clock when I got to the athletic field, almost ninety minutes before our game. All the lines had been painted on the grass by then. I walked past all one hundred yard markers, from goal line to goal line. And every five yards, I'd sink down into my lineman's stance and come exploding forward.

Maybe half our guys were in the locker room changing into their uniforms when I stepped inside, popping the buds from my ears.

Marshall came over to me in his pads and said, "We're going to be a concrete wall today—me, you, and Toby. None of those Park Heights pussies are gonna lay a finger on Ethan."

"None of 'em," I echoed, connecting my fist against his. "Rock solid."

"Steel-reinforced cement," added Toby from in front of his locker, before he downed a Red Bull in one long gulp and then popped the top on another.

I got my equipment together, the white jersey with a big blue 76 on the front and back, my cleats, pants, and shoulder pads. Then I grabbed my white helmet by the face mask and looked at the decals of the growling blue wildcat on the each side. The next time I went out on the field, it wouldn't be just me alone. I'd be one of forty-five, all in the same uniform, ready to prove we were better than those Park Heights losers.

Ethan was sitting by his locker studying the plays printed out on his wristband, with his game face screwed on tight. Godfrey and Bishop had just come back from running wind sprints on the field. They were acting loose, laughing and joking for now.

"Faster than a speeding bullet," announced Godfrey.

"Able to leap tall defenders in a single bound," Bishop added without missing a beat. "It's a bird. It's a plane. No, it's the Wildcat receivers!"

Marshall and Toby had started slamming each other with open palms on the shoulder pads, knocking into lockers, shouting, "How tough?" and answering, "Tougher than tough!"

I got dressed and went into the bathroom to see myself in the full-length mirror on the wall, wearing that uniform. I liked every bit of what I saw. And I felt like some kind of Hercules, ready to lift the world onto my shoulders.

Before we went on the field, Coach made a speech about playing like a team and everybody being on the same page. Then Ethan stood up as team captain and gave a speech of his own.

"We're playing Park Heights tonight," Ethan started out. "The name of their team's the Minutemen. I hear that's what their girlfriends call 'em, too. 'Cause that's all they can last, one measly minute. But they're not even gonna last that long with us. Now, how long is a football game?"

"Sixty minutes!" somebody answered.

"Well, we're gonna roll over their asses inside of the first minute," Ethan said. "And they're gonna have fifty-nine minutes left to be embarrassed."

Ethan stuck his hand out, and we all rushed forward into a big circle to put our hands on top of his. I could feel the pulse of all of them, and I never felt stronger in my life.

"'Wildcats' on three," demanded Ethan. "Ready? One, two, three."

"*Wildcats!*" we all shouted, raising our hands together.

We lined up at the locker room door, till we heard the marching band start to play our fight song.

Then we ran out on the field, crashing through a huge paper banner the cheerleaders were holding from either side. Just before we hit it, I could see the blue wildcat face painted on the front, staring backward at me.

There had to be close to five or six hundred people in the stands. But I found Dad and Mom right away. They were sitting in their usual spot, in the first row behind our team's bench. Jeannie was right beside them, along with Melody and Alan. And if it wasn't for *him* in that damn blue-and-white dress, the same colors my sister and Melody were wearing, it would have been a picture I wanted to keep in a scrapbook.

Our band played the National Anthem, and it was the only time I had my helmet off while I was out there. Then Ethan and Godfrey went out to the middle of the field with the refs and some Park Heights players for the coin toss.

"Heads!" a dude from the other team shouted.

From the sidelines, I saw the coin flipping in the air. After it landed on the ground, Ethan and Godfrey threw their arms up to celebrate. We'd won the toss and elected to receive, going on offense first.

The Park Heights pep squad had a cannon that shot blanks, and a dude dressed up as a minuteman soldier, in a three-cornered hat and knickers, to set it off.

But our mascot, Willie the Wildcat, dressed in a furry wildcat suit, jumped right in front of the cannon, pounded his chest, and wouldn't move.

The crowd went crazy over that, chanting, "Wild-*cats*! Wild-*cats*!"

When our mascot finally moved, that cannon went off with a *boom* as Park Heights kicked us the ball.

It took us ten plays in six minutes on the game clock to drive the ball sixty yards for a touchdown. Our offensive line dominated their D-line on that first series for a 7–0 lead.

Nearly everyone in the stands was stamping their feet and singing to the band's playing.

"We will, we will, rock you!"

Park Heights' players didn't roll over, though. Instead, they got much tougher, and we could hardly budge them after that. But they got real chippy, too, and started taking lots of cheap shots.

The coaches were doing plenty of yelling in our locker room at halftime. Anybody who walked in without knowing the score probably would have thought we were losing.

When Ethan had his turn with the offensive line, he said, "None of you are giving me enough out there. Dominate your man. Cheap-shot 'em right back, just don't get caught. Make 'em wish their mothers never had them."

We went out for the second half pumped up.

But in the third quarter, Park Heights tied the game 7–7, shooting off that damn cannon again in our house.

The next time we were on offense, their biggest defensive player lined up over me. When the ball was snapped, he slapped me hard in the side of the helmet and really rang my bell. He got whistled for a fifteen-yard personal foul, and I was woozy for a few plays.

When I got to the sidelines, I looked over into the stands behind our bench. Everything was spinning a little, and for a few seconds I couldn't tell Jeannie from Melody from Alan, with the three of them wearing blue and white.

That's when our offensive-line coach stuck some smelling salts under my nose. It jolted me, clearing my head in a hurry. And I went back onto the field with the smell of ammonia from those salts still burning the insides of my nostrils.

That dirty Park Heights player who'd cheap-shotted me was in my face again as Ethan barked out signals over center.

"What's the matter, can't take some rough play?" the guy snarled. "This is football, not ballet. You're *supposed* to get hit, homo."

I was breathing fire after he called me that. I wanted to spit in his face so bad.

Then he faked coming over the line. I jumped offsides, too eager to hit him, and I got whistled for a five-yard penalty.

"Fuck that dude—you stay focused!" Marshall yelled at me.

But late in the fourth quarter, with the score still tied, that guy got me to jump again. And this time, it canceled out a good gain by Bishop.

I walked back to the huddle with everybody's eyes on me. I never felt so alone in a circle with ten of my teammates.

"No more stupid mistakes," said Ethan. "Let's get it done."

On the next play, Ethan had Godfrey streaking wide open behind the defense. We blocked the rushers and gave him a perfect pocket to pass from. I could hear the crowd take a deep breath while the ball was in the air.

But Ethan overthrew Godfrey by five yards, and the ball bounced up off the ground into Godfrey's hands.

Alan was cheering in the stands, probably thinking the pass was still good, as he jumped up and down in that dress.

Lots of the Park Heights guys were laughing.

"Is that your new mascot?" one of them cracked. "You the Central High Drag Queens now?"

That got me really pissed off, and I could tell my teammates felt the same way.

Over the next few minutes, we drove the ball down to the one-yard line with enough time left on the clock for one more play.

Ethan called his own number in the huddle—"Fifteen smash," a quarterback-keeper.

I got in my stance and dug my feet into the ground, like I was a tree with roots, making sure not to move until the ball was snapped.

Ethan took the ball and headed around me, on the right side of the line.

I thought he was going to score a touchdown, when suddenly a defender stripped the ball away.

That pigskin rolled right past my big, clumsy feet. All I had to do was fall on it in the end zone to win the game. It was a chance to do my victory dance for real in front of all those people—in front of my parents, and Melody.

But before I could fall on it, a Park Heights player picked up the ball and ran it back the other way, to our end zone.

Their cannon went off just after he'd crossed the goal line.

We'd lost 13 to 7.

Ethan was cursing himself up and down over getting stripped. The rest of us were stone quiet, along with most of the crowd.

A few minutes later, we were lined up in the

middle of the field, shaking hands with the Park Heights players, because that's what our coach made us do.

I was right behind Ethan when that guy who'd slapped me in the head and called me "homo" came up on the line.

He pointed over our shoulders at Alan in the stands and said, "You guys got the ugliest cheerleaders. No wonder you can't win. You should *all* be wearing dresses."

Ethan walked right past the guy without shaking his hand, and so did I.

After that, Ethan started cursing Alan as much as himself for us losing.

ON SATURDAY, I DRAGGED MYSELF AROUND MOST OF THE morning and afternoon, still smarting from that loss the night before. I had half a headache, too, from being slapped in the side of the head by that Park Heights animal. But at around five o'clock, I started getting ready for my date with Melody.

Jeannie was already dressed and heading out before me.

"You got a date tonight?" I asked her.

"Another group thing," she answered.

"With Alan or *Alana*?"

"Yes, and others."

"You know, if you girls want to stop guys from coming up to you, hanging around with him will do the trick."

"Then that wouldn't be the kind of guy I wanted to go out with anyway."

"But that's the only kind there is."

"That's not what Melody would say about you. She says you're kind and considerate, and that your friends don't dictate the way you treat Alan."

"Why do I know that sooner or later he's gonna be the reason Melody decides I'm an idiot. He's gonna lose me her, the same way he helped lose us the game last night."

"You don't *really* believe that, do you?"

"He gave the other team confidence, thinking all our players are *that way*, too."

"Hey, maybe they got confidence when we started singing 'We Will Rock You.' You know that's a song by a band called Queen, and their lead singer was gay and died of AIDS. Ever wonder why they'd even play that song at sporting events?"

"Ha-ha. That's *so* funny, sis."

I had Mom's car again, but I wasn't even thinking about scoring with Melody. Losing our game and not grabbing that loose ball in the end zone kind of dulled me to all of that for now. I'd missed out on one victory dance the night before. So I wasn't going to try for one with Melody, and maybe lose two nights in a row.

Melody's parents were at home this time when I picked her up.

They were both really nice and polite, offering me a soda, asking about my plans for college, and reminding me to drive slow and cautious.

And I tried to match that by calling them "sir" and "ma'am."

But after we left, Melody said to me, "I'm so pissed off at my parents right now. You wouldn't believe the argument I had with them over Alan. They can't stand me being anywhere near him, especially my mother. He was here for two minutes last night before we went to your game. My mother barely met him, and today she says, 'If you hang around him, people are going to think you're perverted, too. And that's a reflection on how we raised you.' Can you believe that?"

"I can understand a little bit where they're coming from," I said.

"You *can*? What about your parents? I know your mom's okay with it. What do you hear from your dad?"

"He's less *okay* with Alan."

"And he tells you about it?"

"We've talked some."

"Well, at least your father sat through a whole football game with him in public. So I know he doesn't question his own masculinity."

"Yeah, Dad's pretty sure of himself. He runs into fires for a living instead of running away from them, like most people."

After a movie that night, I took Melody over to Johnny Rockets for something to eat. The place was a packed, and I had to put my name on a waiting list.

The hostess said it would at least be twenty minutes. But I understood that was restaurant-speak for more like forty minutes.

I saw that Ethan had his name on the list way ahead of mine, for a party of eleven. Him and some of the other guys from the team, and their girlfriends, were hanging out on the benches in front of Rockets, on the inner concourse.

"Do you want to see if we can join them on the list and get seated faster?" I asked Melody on our way back outside, waiting to be called for a table.

"If it's all right, I think I'd rather wait. I kind of get lost in big crowds," said Melody in a hesitant voice. "Hey, would you mind if we went into the Gap for a few minutes, just to look? Kill some time?"

Before I could answer, Toby came up to us, gave me a pound, and said low, "I hope we're not on too long a waiting list to win a game this season."

"Don't worry, we won't be," I told him, giving a thumbs-up to Ethan, who was sitting on a bench with his girlfriend maybe thirty feet away. "Listen, we'll be back in a while, we're going to look at clothes next door."

As we stepped towards the Gap, Toby pointed at the big picture of Gisele Bündchen in the window of Victoria's Secret and said, "You two should go looking next door the other way and see if you can find one of *her* in my size. I'm solo tonight."

I watched Melody's upper lip curl over, like she was biting back something she wanted to say to him.

That's when Jeannie, Maxine, and Alan, who was wearing another dress, stepped out of Rockets. They must have already eaten, because Maxine was carrying a doggie bag.

"Hey, Alana," Ethan called out in a disgusted tone. "You got the lipstick and clothes. When you gonna get yourself a boyfriend?"

"Why, you applying for the job?" Alan shouted back in a heartbeat, with a swish of his hips.

Everyone in earshot was floored by that, and anyone who wasn't on the team was laughing at Ethan.

"I like the name 'Alana.' Call me that anytime you want," said Alan. "And I'll tell you one more thing. There's something in psychology called 'projection.' That's where you put *your* fears on *me*. So maybe it's you who really wants to be walking around dressed this way. And you're just angry that I have the guts to do it and you don't."

"Fuck you, you faggot," snapped Ethan, who was standing up now, with a few of the guys holding him back.

"That's exactly what I'm talking about. You keep saying that out loud, so maybe you'd really like to," responded Alan before he walked away.

11

Sunday afternoon was like an instant replay of Saturday night, with me and Jeannie telling the story of everything that happened from different angles for Mom and Dad in our living room.

"Melody followed after Alan, along with Jeannie and Maxine. And I was stuck there between the guys and them," I said. "Finally, I shrugged my shoulders to Ethan and he says to me, 'Better chase after her 'fore that leash she got tied around your neck chokes the life outta you.'"

"You needed Ethan to tell you it was all right to leave?" asked Jeannie in a sharp tone. "Why? What if he'd told you to stay and sit, like a good little dog? Would you have done that?"

"I don't understand it either Adonis," Mom said,

putting down a section of the Sunday newspaper.

"I do," said Dad, muting the TV to stick up for me. "Ethan's their captain. They're supposed to have each other's backs on the football field. Now I agree, what Ethan said was stupid. But Alan basically called the whole team gay, or at least closet gays. You know they're going to stick together against him. I see why Adonis wasn't going to follow Melody so fast."

"That's right," I said. "I've got to stick together with those guys. They're my teammates."

"But five or six stores down, when Melody called Ethan 'Asshole of the Year,' you didn't stick up for him," Jeannie kept at me.

"Look, it's complicated," I said. "You act like I was the one saying that stuff to Alan. I wasn't. Remember?"

"But you never stood up and said it was wrong," Mom ended it.

Once Melody had seen that Alan was all right and had himself together, she came back and we finally got a table. But Melody was still steamed, and she had lost her appetite. She just sat there pushing the leaves of her salad back and forth while I ate a burger and fries.

"What did you say to those morons, before you caught up to us?" Melody had asked me.

"It all happened so quick, I can't remember exactly," I answered. "But they got the message, loud and clear."

And thanks to Ethan, that bad mood of Melody's didn't get me anything more than a good-night kiss.

For half of Sunday, I was stuck in front of my computer with one eye on pro football and the other on doing D'Antoni's reaction paper on those two stupid poems, due the next day.

One line in the poem that the whole class was doing kept jumping out at me—"Do you suppose yourself advancing on real ground toward a real heroic man?"

And the answer I didn't want to hear was echoing inside my head—*NO!*

But I suffered with that pair of poems long enough to at least get some ideas. And I filled up the one double-spaced typewritten page that I needed, even if I did set the margins short and skipped a couple of lines to start.

On Monday morning, before we handed our papers in, D'Antoni had everybody stand up one at a time and compare their two Whitman poems in just a few sentences.

I was surprised when D'Antoni called Alan, "Alana."

Some kids laughed, even though it didn't sound anything like a joke coming out of D'Antoni's mouth. And I figured Alan and D'Antoni must have talked about using that name before class.

At first, I was pissed that Alan picked the same second poem as me. But a bunch of other kids used "Song of Myself," too. So I don't think anybody else really noticed.

"I think they're both about personal expression. That's why I like a lot of Whitman's work," said Alan. "But the line in our shared poem, 'I am surely far different from what you suppose' That has a lot of meaning to me right now, because of some petition out there against *my* personal expression."

I was waiting for D'Antoni to make a big hippie speech about freedom of choice or something. But he just said, "Thank you for sharing, Alana."

Marshall and Toby both chose "O Captain! My Captain!"

"I like the line in the first poem that says, 'Do you think it so easy to have me become your lover?' Because I want to say to all the *pretty* girls in this school, yes," Marshall said, with a couple of guys, including me, clapping for him. "And in the other poem, Lincoln loves the country so much, he gets killed over it."

"Don't forget the obvious love of the author—a man, for another man, his symbolic captain," said D'Antoni.

"Mr. D'Antoni, no offense, but that's something I try not to think about," said Marshall.

"Honestly, I wouldn't understand why," said D'Antoni, who called on another student before Marshall could say another word.

When it was my turn I said, "I picked this poem because it was one of my mother's favorites. She's a third-grade teacher and says it's about how everybody's the same. Like in the line, 'For every atom belonging to me, as good belongs to you.' But in the other poem it's just the opposite. It says 'take warning—I am surely far different from what you suppose.' So maybe that's how we're the same—we're all different."

D'Antoni looked at me like he was confused.

"Is that *your* idea, Adonis?" he asked.

I nodded my head, waiting for him to correct me. To say how I had it all wrong.

Only it didn't happen.

"That's very insightful," D'Antoni said. "If the rest of your paper's that good, it'll be a sure A."

I was used to sliding by with Cs in English class. So I didn't know how to take it all. But it felt great.

Out of the corner of my eye, I noticed Alan lightly clapping his hands together for me, without making any noise.

MAYBE AN HOUR LATER, BETWEEN MY SECOND- AND THIRD-period classes, I was walking through the hall by the main doors. That's when I saw that sergeant from the military recruiting office setting up a table full of pamphlets and posters. I walked right past him without even thinking about what could happen.

But in the cafeteria, Ethan said to me with a huge grin, "Guess who saw his gay son today for the first time in a dress?"

"The colonel," fell from my mouth.

"You nailed it, bro. Toby and Godfrey were both there when it happened," said Ethan, pointing to them at the table. "Tell Adonis about it. I want to hear it again. I would have given anything to be there."

"I was introducing Godfrey to Colonel Harpring," said Toby. "When all of a sudden the soldier dude's jaw drops, like somebody pulled the pin on a hand grenade and dropped it down his pants."

"Yeah, he must have eagle eyes, 'cause he recognized his faggy flesh and blood in that dress and lipstick from twenty yards down the hall," said Godfrey. "And he went flying over there."

"Of course, we followed him. There was no way we were going to miss seeing the colonel with his *daughter*," said Toby. "They were something like three inches apart, facing each other. They would have been standing chest to chest, if Alana had one."

"'You're a dis-*grace!*' the colonel told him," Godfrey said, making his voice deeper for the imitation. "'An absolute dis-*grace!*'"

Everybody around the table was laughing and giving

high fives. But I had to force a smile for them to see.

Since the start of the semester, Alan had been the biggest pain in the ass. Only it felt too mean to celebrate his father going off on him that way in front of kids.

I thought about the handful of times Dad had completely lost his temper with me. The difference being Dad was never ashamed of who I was, just mad over something dumb I'd done.

"What did he say back?" I asked.

"Nothing. Not a damn word," said Godfrey. "He stood there and took his mouth-whooping like a man—or a woman—till his father turned around and marched straight out of the school."

"Then some of his *girlfriends* put their arms around little Alana, hugging him tight," mocked Toby. "Making sure he didn't break like a china doll."

"Hey, before the colonel left, somebody should have asked him to sign the petition," cackled Ethan. "I'll bet ya he would put down his rank and serial number, too."

All through lunch, I kept that fake smile glued to my face.

Word of what happened spread fast. Later on,

during gym, lots of guys saluted Alan to mess with him, saying shit like, *"Yes, ma'am."*

Alan would snap a salute off right back at them, a few times with just his middle finger. But once, I thought I saw him wipe a tear from his eye, and not sweat.

I was surprised because he'd never shown any real cracks before. But maybe it was harder taking crap from your own father than from somebody like Ethan.

At football practice that afternoon, my teammates mostly fell into two groups: guys who were still hurting so much from us losing on Friday night that they couldn't talk about it, and guys who were ripping Alan—our "ugly cheerleader" and "team jinx"—to shreds for a laugh.

I went through practice keeping my mouth shut, hoping no one would mention me not grabbing that loose ball at the goal line.

No one ever did.

But I stressed over hearing it, over someone accusing me of being the goat in that game, all the way until I left the locker room.

When I got home, Jeannie and Mom were talking

in Jeannie's room again. Only this time the door was open.

"Hey, Adonis, can you come in here?" said Jeannie, her voice cracking. "This concerns you, too."

"Who'd I insult now?" I asked.

"This is about Alan," she said. "You had to hear what happened with his father at school today."

"Yeah, I heard," I said. "Everybody did. It was almost like it was on the loudspeaker with the afternoon announcements."

"It's very sad," Mom said. "I think the colonel should be ashamed of himself."

"Well, Alan's not going home," said Jeannie. "He says he not going to change who he is now. That he can't take that kind of attack from his father ever again. He says he doesn't feel safe, so Maxine invited Alan to stay at her place for a while."

"What are her parents going to say about that?" Mom asked.

"I'm not sure," said Jeannie.

"If it doesn't work out at Maxine's, maybe Child Welfare will place him in a temporary foster home until some of these issues can be resolved," said Mom.

"How about the public shelter with the other homeless people?" I said, thinking I was being helpful.

"No!" said Mom and Jeannie together, their voices almost right on top of each other's.

"Adonis, a shelter could be dangerous for him," continued Mom.

"Why don't you ask him to sleep in the football team's weight-lifting trailer?" mocked Jeannie. "I'm sure he'd be just as safe there."

"All right, can I take any more abuse here?" I said. "Look, I admit I feel kind of sorry for him. But exactly how does this concern me, Jeannie?"

"Because," said Jeannie. "I think eventually we should ask him to stay here."

I was so floored by that I couldn't even open my mouth to respond.

Nightmare scenes were flying through my head so fast I couldn't find my place in any of them for more than a split second. But I knew they all had to do with people pointing at me, and me being pinned down, crushed, between my teammates and Melody, between everything normal and Queer City.

"No," said Mom, firm. "I'm sorry, Jeannie. But absolutely not."

I heard that and finally I could feel my legs and feet beneath me again.

"But why?" asked Jeannie with her emotions rising.

"Honey, this family's already involved in helping Alan," Mom said. "He's your friend. We accept him and support him. And I'm very proud of all you've done. But we can't come between Alan and his father. They're going to have to work things out for themselves. Having him stay here with us would make our relationship with him too important. I can't allow it. It wouldn't be healthy for any of us, including Alan."

"Mom's right," I said. "It would turn our whole lives upside down."

"That's not exactly what I meant," Mom told me.

"I know, just that it wouldn't work out," I said. "It would be crazy here."

"I can't believe you'd turn your back on Alan like

this," Jeannie complained to Mom. "You always taught me to help people, especially when—"

Jeannie pulled up short on her words and threw a little tantrum, marching out of her own room.

That left me looking at Mom, like we were the two adults.

ALAN WAS AT SCHOOL TUESDAY, WEARING THE SAME OUTFIT he'd had on the day before. But other than that, you couldn't tell he was semi-homeless. Alan smiled on and off. He sat with his back straight and raised his hand high every time he had something to say. Either he was the toughest girl-guy I'd ever seen, or it was one big front to hide his feelings.

Before the end of class, D'Antoni gave our reaction papers back. There was an *A*+ sitting in the top right-hand corner of mine, along with the comment "Outstanding Interpretation!" It was refrigerator-magnet material for props at home from Mom and Dad, and maybe a faster track to my own decent set of wheels before my eighteenth birthday in December. Only I couldn't believe I'd got that kind of grade figuring out the poems of D'Antoni's hippie king, Walt Whitman.

After football practice that day, Ethan got everyone together in the locker room.

"I asked the student council to hold a pep rally this week for the team," Ethan said. "Our game Friday night is on the road at Utica, so we're not going to get nearly as many people in the stands pulling for us. They agreed we deserve the support, so they're working on something for this Thursday night at the Tri-County Mall. But they said we might have to share it with the Fashion Club, because they'd been asking for an event this week, too."

"Yeah, yeah, hot females!"

"Woo, woo!"

"No problemo!"

Then somebody yelled out, "What about that freak in a dress, our damn jinx? Is he gonna be there, too?"

"Hopefully not, so we won't have to look at that misfit," Ethan said, cold. "If we do get stuck with Alana there, I may have a real public answer. I can't comment yet because the wheels are still turning in my head. But you can bet, if we get embarrassed, so will *she*. And it'll be sweet . . . really sweet."

I didn't feel good about it, but I clapped and cheered along with everyone else when Ethan was finished.

12

That Tuesday night, Jeannie wasn't at home for family dinner.

"I gave her permission to eat at Maxine's house tonight," Mom told Dad and me, as I set the table alone. "With Alan not living at home right now, lots of her friends are going to be having him over for dinner. And we'll take our turn, too."

"It's not that I'm unsympathetic, but it's amazing to me how other people's problems cut into *our* family time," said Dad. "And now I'm carrying part of the load for that colonel's bad parenting."

"You don't think having Alan here for dinner is a bad idea, like what you were talking about, getting between him and his father?" I asked Mom.

"No, I don't," she answered.

"Nice try, son," said Dad with a laugh. "I was a hundred percent behind you on that one. I've had enough of all this drama, too."

"But I am proud of you, Adonis," Mom said. "You've put the knives and forks on the correct sides of the plates for once."

"Well, then you'll be even prouder of this," I said, pulling my English paper out of my pocket and unfolding it in front of them.

"Whoa, in English, an A-plus—that's terrific," Mom gushed. "See, poetry's not some foreign language. It's about feelings and perspective, just like life."

"Our varsity athlete, lover boy, poetry critic," said Dad. "What a combination."

"I guess there's not too many of them," I said.

"What you're doing's all right with me, as long as you never try on any of your sister's clothes," said Dad with a grin, before Mom tapped him on back of the head.

THE NEXT DAY IN SCHOOL, WEDNESDAY, I SAW MELODY IN the hall between classes. She greeted me with a big, sexy smile and pulled me over into a corner.

"I'm so excited," she said. "We're doing a fashion show as part of the pep rally at Tri-County tomorrow night, and I'm modeling. Now you can cheer for me, and I can cheer for you. Because God knows, you're about the only one left on that football team of idiots I can support."

"I know, it was insane with those guys and Alan on Saturday," I said. "I don't know how to apologize for them."

"Oh, it's 'Alana' now, no more 'Alan,'" Melody said. "Promise me you'll do whatever you can to make your teammates back off, especially at the rally and show."

"I'll try my absolute best," I told her. "I can't wait to see you model. What are you going to be wearing?"

"I don't even know yet—we have to figure it all out at our meeting today."

As she walked away, I thought about her strutting her stuff in front of the whole team, with every guy there thinking, *She's Adonis's girl. That hot honey's with Adonis.*

And that had me totally pumped up.

At lunch, Ethan didn't mention any details about him getting even with Alana.

He just told the guys at our table, "It's on for tomorrow night, the pep rally, the Fashion Club show, everything. And I mean *everything*."

Godfrey and Bishop pressed him for more info, only Ethan wouldn't budge.

"I can't chance any details getting out there. I'll keep you all informed on a need-to-know basis," said Ethan, like some kind of military commander.

That was fine with me. I left there with a full stomach, feeling good about myself that I didn't really know a thing about his plan.

Later on, I even nodded my head to Alan when we came face-to-face with each other during gym class. My conscience was clear about anything that was going to happen, because I could tell myself I had no idea what it was.

But in a little more than an hour, I couldn't use that excuse anymore.

———

AT PRACTICE, INSIDE OF OUR FIRST HUDDLE, ETHAN PULLED US together around him tight and said, "Here's the secret play, for our ears only. Melissa Henry donated one of her old cheerleading sweaters to the cause. She's gonna sew big, fake boobs into it. Right before the end of the fashion show, me, Marshall, and Toby will come out in masks. I'll shove the sweater over queer boy's head. Then Marshall will plop a long, blonde wig on him. Toby's there to run interference, in case anybody gets in the way. I'm calling it 'The Blindsided Double-Reverse.' The rest of you know it's coming, so help out any way you can in the crowd. Now—ready, break!"

Ethan clapped his hands, and we all moved up to the line of scrimmage.

I sank down into my offensive lineman's stance beside with Marshall and Toby, and waited for Ethan to bark out our signals.

I was surprised at what was going through my mind. Yes, I was worried about getting caught on the other side of the line from Melody and my sister, how it would reflect on me and what it might cost me. But deep down, I was even more worried about Alan.

AT HOME THAT NIGHT, JEANNIE WAS PRACTICING HER PART IN the fashion show for Mom in the living room when I walked in.

"So as president and vice president, Alana and I are taking turns as master of ceremonies. We'll do the opening together, Alana will do the second part, I'll do the third, and then we'll do one more part together," Jeannie told Mom before I interrupted.

"Is that the end, with you two standing up there together?" I asked.

"No, Alana ends the show by thanking the members of the Fashion Club for all their hard work," Jeannie answered with some attitude. "Why, are you afraid the last thing your football friends will see before the pep rally is Alana and me together?"

"No, that's not it," I said. "This is all going to be on the inner concourse, right?"

"By the Gap and Victoria's Secret. Both stores are

donating some clothes, and Rockets is running a special on food for anyone with a Central High student ID," said Jeannie.

"I'm just trying to picture it all clear in my head. It's my pep rally, too," I said. "Besides, I want to know when your part's finished, so I can go up and congratulate you."

"I'm impressed, Adonis," Mom said. "You're valuing other people's hard work. That's an important quality to have."

"Yeah, I'll bet," mocked Jeannie. "Melody probably told him she has that kind of relationship with *her* brother."

"I think Adonis deserves a little more consideration than that," Mom stuck up for me. "He's come a long way lately, with the idea of Alana hanging around here and everything else."

I'd already turned around and was heading up the stairs when I heard Jeannie say, "Maybe—maybe I'm wrong. I'm sorry, Adonis."

"It's okay," I muttered from over my shoulder.

———

MY EYES OPENED IN THE DARKNESS, WITH JUST THE GREEN fluorescent glow of the numbers on a clock radio to see by. I was exhausted and wanted to go back to sleep. But my bladder felt like it was about to explode. So I dragged myself out of bed and staggered down the hall.

The smell of perfume was everywhere, like Jeannie or Mom had spilled a whole bottle of it on the hallway carpet.

But the floor still felt dry beneath my shuffling bare feet.

I looked up at the bathroom door and there was a small sign with a figure on it. One side of that figure was a man and the other side was a woman in a triangle skirt. Right away, I thought Jeannie was playing some kind of dumb joke.

Reaching for the doorknob, a chill ran through me as it turned open on its own.

Alan stepped out, without paying a bit of attention to me.

He was wearing a cheerleader sweater stuffed with gigantic, fake boobs.

Then, raising a pair of blue-and-white pom-poms high over his head, he gave a school cheer.

"Central High! Central High! Our Wildcat growl is do or die!"

After that, Alan strutted past me down the hall, like he was on the runway in a fashion show.

Melody walked out of the bathroom next, in a killer minidress. She blew me a kiss good-bye off the palm of her hand and strutted behind Alan.

Suddenly, I was staring into the bathroom mirror.

Dad was standing at attention beside me, and Colonel Harpring was behind him, barking out orders.

My dirty football uniform was piled up in front of me in the sink, and I was struggling to get it on fast.

"Move your pathetic ass, soldier!" the colonel screamed. "Football's a man's game. It's a ground war, and you've got to have your teammates' backs!"

Only no matter how hard I struggled to get dressed, my uniform wouldn't fit.

Finally, the colonel shoved me out into the hallway, hollering, "You're a disgrace, son. A disgrace to that uniform! Get out there as you are!"

I was completely naked, running late for the game or the pep rally.

I didn't know which.

But Mom and Jeannie were on my tail now, chasing me down the stairs, yelling, "What did you know, Adonis? What did you know?"

That's when my eyes popped up in bed for *real*, with my heart racing.

I was drenched in a cold sweat, with the blanket and sheets soaking wet.

LATER THAT THURSDAY MORNING, I SKIPPED BREAKFAST AND managed to get out of the house without making eye contact with Mom or Jeannie. Only Barclay had shadowed me around, until I opened him a fresh can of stinky dog food.

Alan was there in D'Antoni's class, along with Marshall and Toby, who'd both caught my eye a few times. They'd jut their jaws at Alan's back, and then grin at me and each other, probably over Ethan's plan.

Part of me wished I could pull Alan aside. I'd tell him that the team didn't want him anywhere near our pep rally. That he'd already won round one with Ethan that night outside of Rockets. That he should quit while he was ahead, before anything *really* stupid happened and somebody got hurt.

But in my mind, the distance between my seat and his was enough of an excuse to walk away from that feeling.

Then, right before the end of class, D'Antoni said, "Everybody get into your groups. For the final step of your spoils project, I need you to discuss creating your team's logo."

Inside of a minute, I was sitting in a small circle of desks with Alan, Maxine, and Wendy. I listened as they did most of the talking, kicking around ideas for a logo design.

"Like I mentioned before, we could work one of those fire dogs, a Dalmatian, into it," said Maxine. "And you know what, black and white's never out of style, and those two colors go with anything."

"You're always tuned into fashion, Max," said Alan.

"How about a fireman's helmet in place of a football helmet?" asked Wendy.

"Good. That works, too," said Alan, pushing the right sleeve on his blouse back up to his elbow to match the left side. "And don't forget about a football."

After we'd all admitted that none of us could draw worth a damn, Alan said, "Let's all take a try at it. We can either hand in the best one, or four terrible ones."

I nodded my head to him. And then before I'd even realized the words had left my mouth, I'd asked, "How are you doing at Maxine's?"

"I'm getting by, Adonis. Thank you for asking," he responded through a pair of bright red lips.

"He's a pleasure to have as a guest," added Maxine.

"For now she says that. But what's that old saying? Fish and company stink after three days," said Alan. "Anyway, Adonis, I don't know how many football players will arrive early for fashion show tonight. But I'll ask the entire Fashion Club to stay afterward for the pep rally to cheer your team on."

"I know all about it," I said with my mind wandering.

"You do?" Alan asked, sounding confused. "How?"

"I mean, thanks," I answered, focusing again. "We could use the extra support."

And I choked back down everything else another part of me wanted to tell him.

13

I ate lunch alone at a side table away from Ethan and the guys, with my nose buried inside a book. In my head, I had a few excuses ready about why I was sitting alone.

I'm cramming for an exam.

I've got a big book report due.

My group's way behind on D'Antoni's sports project.

But I was surprised when none of my teammates came over to find out what was going on with me, and I didn't have to use any of those lines.

Later on, in gym class, I stayed as far away from Alan as I could, trying to block what I knew about Ethan's plan completely out of my mind.

Only that turned out to be as hard as blocking out

any 250-pound rhino who ever lined up against me on the football field.

The team practiced without pads that afternoon, running the first fifteen offensive plays we had scripted for our game against Utica the next night.

Inside our huddles, Ethan was all business, never mentioning anything other than football.

"I'm sick of being called a loser. And all of you should be, too," Ethan preached. "It's in our hands, and it ends right here. Winners execute their plans to perfection. That's what we're going to concentrate on."

Marshall and Toby, along with everyone else, followed his lead.

"You heard our captain," said Marshall. "It's all about winning. The rest is for chumps, and that's not us."

Practice ended at around four thirty, but I didn't want to go home.

The pep rally didn't start until six fifteen, and me and Jeannie both had permission from Dad to miss family dinner. So I hit the showers at the far end of the locker room. Then I went out to the trailer to lift some weights. Two or three other guys were there at first, but after about fifteen minutes, I was all alone.

I stared into the mirrored wall, squatting beneath a heavy load with no one to spot for me. I did six reps, straining more with each one.

On the seventh rep, I felt my knees begin to buckle.

Then I lost my balance a little bit, and thought I might even fall over.

"Hold it together," I told myself. "You can do it."

I worked to steady myself and drove harder with my legs to get it under control. Right before I stood up straight to finish the rep, I wanted to drop that weight off my chest and shoulders and walk away. But I guess I liked what I saw in that mirror too much to let go.

I took the long walk over to the Tri-County Mall, with a dull ache rippling through my thighs and hamstrings.

The mall's inner concourse was loud, jam-packed with kids from our school. They were camped out on the benches, sitting at Rockets' patio tables downing dollar sodas and two-dollar burger specials for Central High students, or standing around a portable stage with dark curtains that was positioned in the middle of everything.

As the music kicked in, everyone began to cheer. And that's when Jeannie and Alan stepped out from behind those curtains to start the fashion show.

They were standing close together, sharing the one microphone to take turns speaking.

"Thanks to the Tri-County Mall for sponsoring the Central High Fashion Club's first official fashion show," said Alan, who was wearing a checkered blouse I'd seen on Jeannie at least a dozen times.

He got mostly cheers, but there were some boos and whistles mixed in, too.

"And special thanks to our student body for coming out to support us today, and the pep rally for the Central High Wildcats football team to follow," announced Jeannie in an excited voice, with the audience already cheering. "Now, do you want to see some fashion? Let's get started."

I noticed Ethan, Marshall, and Toby standing together, maybe fifty feet away from me. The three of them were dressed in their team jackets. And when the girls stepped out to model, they cheered along with the rest of the crowd.

Then, halfway through the show, I watched them leave.

A moment later, Melody came out for her turn on the stage.

The music was blaring—"Feeling hot, hot, hot."

Guys all around me were hooting and hollering for her. Suddenly, it felt like it was a hundred degrees in the mall and I was starting to really sweat.

I looked at Melody's legs and waist, with my eyes getting up as high as her chest. But I couldn't look Melody in the face, not with what I knew was about to let happen.

Jeannie and Alan switched places a few times on the microphone. And I was worried that Jeannie could get hurt if she got in the way.

Right before the fashion show was over, I saw Ethan, Marshall, and Toby come back inside, following behind some cheerleaders. They were bent over low, walking with their heads down. They'd ditched the team jackets and their faces were hidden behind animal masks—Ethan's a dog, Marshall's and Toby's pigs.

I recognized Ethan by his sneakers, because I was wearing the exact same brand.

And as they got closer to the stage, so did I.

As Alan began to thank people, with Jeannie taking care of something over by the curtains, Ethan leaped onto the stage holding that cheerleader sweater with the big boobs sewn inside.

Then Ethan went to pull it down over Alan's head.

Only Alan wasn't going to stand for it.

Maybe Ethan couldn't see much through that dog mask. But Alan caught him flush on the jaw with a straight right hand.

That's when Toby and Marshall rushed the stage. I jumped up there, too, to keep between them and Jeannie, who I knew would fight for Alan.

Ethan had gone down in a heap from that punch.

But Marshall came at Alan with a long blonde wig.

Alan kicked him hard in the shin with the toe of his

pointed shoe, and I could almost feel the sharp pain in my own shin as Marshall went down.

Then Toby grabbed Alan from behind.

Ethan got back up to his feet and came at Alan again.

I intercepted Jeannie, stopping her from getting in the middle of it.

That's when Alan got an arm free, and somehow yanked Ethan's mask off in front of everyone.

The air was vibrating with screams, cheers, and gasps.

It felt like there was an earthquake rumbling beneath me, rolling up my entire body, shaking me to the core.

Ethan punched Alan in the head as Toby held him.

I saw Alan's eyes roll back, and could feel Jeannie's scream from inside my arms.

Then Ethan wound up his fist again, while Alan was out of it and defenseless.

That's what it took to get me to move—to cross that line.

I let go of Jeannie and got to Alan just after that second punch landed on his skull.

I knocked Ethan flat with a block that he never saw

coming. And when I dropped him, it felt like I'd finally dropped some kind of heavy load I'd been struggling with for way too long.

After that, I wrestled Toby down, keeping one eye on Marshall, who was still on the floor.

Alan was stretched out cold, and I heard the voices around him now yelling, "Get an ambulance! Call 911!"

Before any kind of medical help arrived, Alan opened his eyes and came to.

He didn't speak, and didn't seem to really know where he was.

There were sighs of relief from everyone huddled around him, including me.

Eventually, I knew I was going to have a lot to explain.

Melody thought I was some kind of hero for what I did, and so did Jeannie.

Only I didn't deserve any of that.

I played it down as much as I could, and even told them, "I should have done more. You don't know it, but I should have."

The EMTs took Alan to Mercy Hospital, and the cops hauled Ethan, Marshall, and Toby away in handcuffs.

LATER THAT NIGHT, AT AROUND TEN THIRTY, DAD AND MOM drove Jeannie and me to the hospital. One of the nurses told us Alan had suffered a severe concussion, and that Colonel Harpring was in Alan's room with him.

When Alan's father heard that we were there, he asked for the two of us to come inside.

Jeannie attached herself to my arm, and we entered together.

Alan was in bed, resting with his eyes closed and his head bandaged. He was dressed in a white hospital gown, and the red lipstick had been cleaned off his mouth.

"I want to thank you for protecting my son," the colonel said low, extending his hand to me. "You're more of a friend to him than those Fashion Clubbers who indulged him in his need to stand out and cause controversy."

Jeannie let that remark go and asked in a quiet voice, "How is he? Will he be all right?"

"He's been groggy, with a bad headache and some vomiting. I think he's finally asleep. They took an MRI and didn't see any damage to his brain. But the doctors say they need to keep him for at least a two-day observation period," the colonel told us. "Now that this situation has settled a little bit, the soldier in me is thinking how I'd like to wring the necks of those boys who attacked Alan."

"I'll bet part of it's the father in you, too," said Jeannie. "Besides, the police have got those animals where they belong now—in a cage. I don't like fighting, but Adonis gave them something they really deserved."

That's when I turned my face away from them, and I saw my reflection framed inside the windowpane. It was thin and nearly transparent against the dark night sky. Both my hands were buried inside my pockets as I wondered what kind of bars I should be behind for keeping my mouth shut and letting that damn attack happen.

"You were plenty brave tonight in doing what you

did," the colonel said, dropping a hand onto my shoulder. "You know, you'd probably make a good soldier, Adonis."

"Thanks, sir, but I don't think so," I answered, looking his military duds up and down. "I've had enough of uniforms for a while."

"Well, you seem to be on the right track in life. One I wish *my* son were on," he said, moving towards the door. "Anyway, I'm going to speak to the doctors one last time before I leave for the night. I just wanted you to fully understand my appreciation."

After the colonel left, Jeannie gently stroked Alan's hand.

"It's not fair that all these people have an opinion on who Alana should be," said Jeannie. "It doesn't concern any of them. It doesn't. Look at what it made them do."

"I see it now," I said. "It's garbage."

That's when Jeannie pulled a small bottle of perfume from her pocket, the same perfume she'd loaned Alan more than a week before.

She tried her best to open it, but the lid was stuck tight.

I took the bottle from her hands and used all my strength to twist off the top.

Then I walked over to watch the door, checking for the colonel, as Jeannie put a drop behind Alan's left ear.

14

When we got home from the hospital, I confessed to my family that I'd known the attack on Alan was coming. I did it in the living room, almost the second we'd walked through the front door. I had to. I couldn't keep it inside of me any longer.

Jeannie was the hardest on me.

"I want to know this," she demanded. "If Alan wasn't wearing lipstick and women's clothes, would you have let it go that far? Would you? Would you have let the three of them attack somebody half their size if he wasn't *different?*"

"I guess not," I said, though I knew it wasn't nearly enough. "I'm sorry. I really screwed up. I just felt like I couldn't rat out my friends."

"That's who you call friends?" mocked Jeannie.

"I'm more than disappointed in that decision, Adonis," chided Mom. "That should have been no choice for you at all."

"You're right," I told her, feeling smaller than I could ever remember. "Like I said, I really screwed up."

"It's true, you screwed up in a way. But you also might have saved Alan's life tonight," said Dad. "Let's not forget about that."

"If Adonis had just said something, he wouldn't have had to save anybody's life," argued Jeannie.

"He was trying to stay out of it by keeping quiet," explained Dad.

"That's exactly what I tried to do," I said as my only line of defense.

"*Tried?*" questioned Jeannie. "Not the way I see it."

"Maybe you want to make your brother out to be more guilty than he is," said Dad. "Adonis wasn't wearing a mask. He wasn't on that stage to attack anyone. He's not in handcuffs. And I've got a problem with anyone who thinks he's the same as those other boys."

"It's true, there are different degrees of guilt," added

Mom. "But in my eyes, you're a long way from blameless, Adonis."

"I can't wait till he explains it to Melody," said Jeannie, with some real venom.

"I don't know if I can do that," I said as the weight of it settled on my shoulders.

"Better Melody hears it from your mouth than someone else's," said Mom. "And if you don't tell her first thing tomorrow, you'll be putting pressure on your sister to lie for you. That's not right."

"I won't lie for him, not even by keeping quiet," said Jeannie. Our living room was turning into battleground, and I was getting destroyed. "That's the same game that got Alana a concussion."

Then Jeannie punctuated those words with her pounding footsteps as she headed up the stairs.

I hardly got a wink of sleep that night, worrying about Alan and how I'd break the news to Melody. I was exhausted in the morning and woke up feeling twice as bad. And in the half hour it took me to tiptoe around breakfast and get out of the house, Barclay was the only one to treat me normally.

Just before first period, I spotted Melody in the hall outside of D'Antoni's classroom. I walked straight up to her and spilled my guts.

She stamped her foot on the floor, harder and harder in a fit of rage, before she finally got ahold of herself and screamed, "I can't believe this! No! You weren't supposed to be like them! I'm so stupid!"

As Melody left me standing there alone, Maxine ran out of the room after her.

She caught up to Melody halfway down the hall, and I slunk inside to take my seat. Maxine didn't get back to class until a few minutes after the late bell. But I knew that Melody must have filled her in on everything, because for the rest of the period Maxine was staring daggers at me.

"Fraud," she mouthed in my direction, during D'Antoni's lesson.

Other kids had heard Melody's explosion, too, and probably picked up on Maxine's stares. I felt like every one of them had their eyes on me. And the only empty seats in English class that morning belonged Toby, Marshall, and Alan.

From the second I got to school, kids had been all over me.

They were either congratulating me for putting Ethan in his place, or looking at me like a traitor for going against my teammates. Anybody on the football team who might have cut me an inch of slack for protecting Alan was already blaming me for another losing season, thinking those guys would get suspended for sure.

"You cost us our starting quarterback and half the offensive line, for what?"

"Are you going to play all those positions by yourself, Adonis?"

"We'll be lucky to win one game without those guys."

And now with Melody, Maxine, and Jeannie spreading the word about me to their Fashion Club friends, that I'd known about the attack and had done nothing to stop it, I wasn't going to have many supporters left.

I skipped my lunch period, wanting to avoid Godfrey and Bishop around that half-empty table.

Instead, I hid out in the library where I wouldn't have to say a word to anyone, and that old-as-dust lady librarian would protect me with a finger over her lips and a tense *shhh*.

But Melody had more to say, and later on she tracked me down in the hallway between classes.

"I want you to understand this, Adonis," she said, her eyes drilling into mine. "Right now, I have no idea who you are or what you're about. I don't know how much you told me about Alana or anything else was a lie, and how much was reality. But I can't keep friends like that. They're worthless. Do you get it?"

I nodded my head and muttered, "I'm really sorry," as she walked off.

For a moment, I thought I was going to break down and bawl right there.

Not over the thought of Melody never wanting to date me again—I expected that.

But over the idea that I wasn't good enough to be her friend anymore. And that word *worthless* settled into the pit of my stomach and began to ache.

I managed to drag my ass through gym class, open-ing and closing it out with a long, slow jog around the red rubber track where I'd first laid eyes on Alan.

When I got home, no one else was there.

Jeannie had left a note on the fridge:

Called hosp. Alana feeling much better, going to visit. —J

Her note was hanging next to my A-plus paper on that pair of Walt Whitman poems.

Staring me in the face was a sentence of mine that D'Antoni had circled and written the word *YES!* next to. It read: *I think Whitman was trying to say that we're all the same not because we're just like each other but because we're all different from each other.*

I GOT BACK TO SCHOOL AT EXACTLY FOUR THIRTY, THE LATEST I could report to the locker room for a road game.

"Nobody here blames you for Ethan," said Godfrey

as I gathered up my gear. "It was that she-dude who ripped his mask off. We just blame you for Marshall and Toby getting nailed."

"Yeah, you're never supposed to fight against teammates for someone else," said Bishop. "How can we trust you on the field now to have our backs against whoever? And what makes you think we're going to have *your* back now?"

"I guess I can't be sure," I answered. "I just want to know this: if Ethan had picked you two, instead of Marshall and Toby, would you have done it?"

"Why you want to know something like that?" snapped Godfrey.

"He's probably been asking himself the same damn question. That's why," added Bishop.

He was right. I had. Only I wasn't 100 percent sure of the answer I'd come up with.

Hardly anyone said a word to me on the bus ride to Utica.

As part of our pregame speech, Coach told us that Ethan, Marshall, and Toby had been suspended from the football team for the rest of the season. That all three of them were facing charges, had posted bail, and now had to deal with some kind of principal's suspension before they could even come back to school.

The thought of eventually seeing those guys at school rattled me a little. But I figured I was going to have a tougher time facing Alan than any of them.

Dad came to the game by himself. He was probably the only one in the stands rooting for me.

We started a sophomore at quarterback, and two freshmen on the offensive line. It was a disaster from the start as we turned the ball over with interceptions and fumbles, and dug ourselves a deep 21–0 hole. And the worst part of that beating was that thirty minutes of football took a little more than an hour and a half to play.

At halftime, I sat alone on a bench, listening to Coach pound us for our mistakes. But I knew most of the players in that locker room blamed me.

I kept my eyes down on the dark blue tiled floor.

It was like being stranded alone on a tiny island in

the middle of a shark-filled ocean, with every wave of criticism washing away any ground I had left to stand on.

The second half of football was more pitiful for us than the first, and the final score was Utica 49, Central High 0.

Afterwards, we were lined up on the field shaking hands with the Utica players when one of my teammates mocked, "Hi, my name's Adonis. I have a gay friend and I personally gift-wrapped this game for you."

I'd heard enough and I decided not to take the team bus home. I didn't even tell any of the coaches. I just found Dad and said, "Let's go."

"You want to drive?" he asked, dangling the keys to the Trans Am.

"Why, is that the booby prize?" I said. "I'll probably wreck it like I did the team. No, thanks."

On the way home, Dad said, "I'm still proud of you. I understand why you didn't stop Ethan and the rest of them before it happened, or even warn Alan. You don't have to think for anyone else, just yourself. And when you saw they'd gone way overboard, you put an end to it. I don't know what more anyone can ask."

"That's what I thought going in," I said. "But it didn't feel that way when it was over. And I didn't need Jeannie or Mom or Melody to tell me."

"They're your feelings. You're entitled. I'm happy to know what they are. It's more than I had with my father," said Dad. "Hey, remember my favorite wrestler, "Adorable" Adrian Adonis?"

"You mean the one I'm partly named after?"

"Yeah. Well, he died more than twenty years ago in a car accident. He swerved to avoid hitting a moose in the road and lost control."

"Really?"

"He began his career as a biker-type brawler, wearing a leather jacket in the ring. But then he changed his gimmick."

"To what?"

"Out of nowhere, he bleached his hair blond, started dressing in pink, and wore women's clothes for his matches."

"No way. You're making that up."

"I'm not. It's the God's honest truth. That's how he got the nickname 'Adorable.' He even hosted a segment called *The Flower Shop* on a wrestling TV show."

"But it wasn't for real. It was just a put-on, an act for ratings, right?"

"I think so."

"So did he stop being your favorite wrestler after that?"

"No, I still rooted for him. I just didn't tell as many people."

Even after finding all that stuff out, I wasn't embarrassed to be named after him.

When we got home, Mom didn't have to ask the score. She could read it on my face.

"Start on whatever schoolwork you have for the weekend," she said as I headed up to my room. "It'll take your mind off it."

That's when I remembered the team logo for our sports project.

I'd never planned on drawing one, because I knew somebody else's would be much better. But I didn't need Maxine or anyone else pointing at it as one more thing I should have done for Alan.

So I pencil-sketched a Dalmatian the best I could, using Barclay for a model and adding the spots and long ears. Then I drew a fire helmet on the Dalmatian's head, with its paw holding up a football to be kicked.

It wasn't a work of art, but at least I could say I did my share.

On Saturday, I didn't want to get out of bed and slept till almost noon.

There was no way I was going to lift weights with my teammates.

Then I looked in the mirror and wondered if I even wanted to play football anymore.

When I finally made it downstairs, I didn't know what to do with myself.

"You want to help me do some gardening?" Mom asked me.

"No, I can't stand the smell of fertilizer," I answered. "Anyway, isn't that you and Jeannie's together thing?"

"Your sister went down to the hospital with some

of her friends," she said. "I understand Alana's being released later on today. I just don't know if she's going home or to Maxine's."

Fifteen minutes later, I found myself on the city bus, heading to Mercy Hospital.

I had no idea what I was going to say when I got there. And I didn't want to plan it out ahead of time and try to make myself sound any more than what I was—sorry.

When I came off the hospital elevator, I saw Alan's room right away.

It was filled with flowers and visitors—Jeannie, Maxine, and Melody.

I knocked at the open door and the room turned silent.

"Adonis, what brings you here?" asked Alan, breaking the ice.

"I came to see you," I answered in a soft tone.

Jeannie said to her friends, "Maybe we should leave them alone for a while."

As Melody passed me on her way out, she gave me a look with a lot less anger in her eyes.

Then, suddenly, it was just Alan and me, face-to-face.

He was wearing a white hospital gown and bright red lipstick. And I couldn't tell if he had on perfume or if it was the scent of all the flowers that found my nostrils.

A nurse walked in and saw us together.

"Excuse me," she said, before grabbing a chart and leaving.

I guess she could have thought that I was Alan's boyfriend. But that didn't matter to me now.

"I suppose I should start off by thanking you," said Alan. "I heard from the girls that despite knowing about the attack, you showed a lot of courage that night."

"No. You were the one who showed all the real courage. And that was from the beginning," I said in what felt like the most honest voice I'd used in a long time. "I was the scared one. I was scared of what people would think. And that fear got to be much bigger than what I thought about myself. I was wrong. I was wrong about you and about me. Maybe we can just start over again, if you can ever forgive me."

"Sure."

"I'm Adonis," I said, extending my hand, to shake on a new friendship.

"I'm Alana."

Are You the New Person Drawn Toward Me?

by Walt Whitman

(1819–1892)

Are you the new person drawn toward me?
To begin with take warning, I am surely far different
  from what you suppose;
Do you suppose you will find in me your ideal?
Do you think it so easy to have me become your
  lover?
Do you think the friendship of me would be unalloy'd
  satisfaction?
Do you think I am trusty and faithful?
Do you see no further than this façade—this
  smooth and tolerant manner of me?
Do you suppose yourself advancing on real ground
  toward a real heroic man?
Have you no thought O dreamer that it may be all
  maya, illusion?

Excerpts from "Song of Myself"

I celebrate myself, and sing myself,
And what I assume you shall assume,
For every atom belonging to me as good belongs
    to you.

I loafe and invite my soul,
I lean and loafe at my ease observing a spear of
    summer grass.

My tongue, every atom of my blood, form'd from
    this soil, this air,
Born here of parents born here from parents the
    same, and their parents the same, . . .

Houses and rooms are full of perfumes, the shelves
    are crowded with perfumes,
I breathe the fragrance myself and know it and
    like it,
The distillation would intoxicate me also, but I shall
    not let it.

The atmosphere is not a perfume, it has no taste of the distillation, it is odorless,

It is for my mouth forever, I am in love with it,

I will go to the bank by the wood and become undisguised and naked,

I am mad for it to be in contact with me.